CYNTHIA THOMPSON

THE
POWER
OF A
PROPHETIC
MINDSET

The Power of a Prophetic Mindset
© Copyright 2014 – Cynthia Thompson

All rights reserved. No part of this book may be reproduced, stored in a retrieval system, or transmitted in any form or by any means- electronic, mechanical, photocopying, recording, or otherwise, without prior written permission of the copyright owner, except by a reviewer who wishes to quote brief passages in connection with a review for inclusion in a magazine, newspaper, or broadcast.

Biblical scripture quotations are taken from King James, NIV, The Message and Amplified Bibles, unless otherwise stated. All emphasis within scripture quotations is the author's own.

International Standard Book Number:
978-0-9894680-3-9

Design by Shaquille Coleby

**FOR SPEAKING ENGAGEMENTS
AND MORE INFORMATION ABOUT
ETERNAL CHANGE MINISTRIES
AND THE PROPHETIC TRAINING CENTER
CALL: (561) 361-0610
EMAIL: prophetcynthia@prophetictrainingcenter.com
WEBSITE: www.eternalchangeministries.org**

Published by
Divine Works Publishing
Wellington, Florida 33414
(561) 247-1359
info@divineworkspublishing.com

Table of Contents

Endorsements v

Foreword ix

Dedication x

Introduction xiv

Chapter 1 The Human Mind 1

Chapter 2 Transformation of the Mind 7

Chapter 3 Understanding the Prophetic 15

Chapter 4 Cultivating a Prophetic Mindset 21

Chapter 5 A Higher Way of Thinking 35

Chapter 6 The Prophetic Spirit 47

Chapter 7 The Mind of Prophecy 57

Chapter 8 Prophetic Prayer 65

Prophetic Declarations 77

2014 Prophetic Words 79

Endorsements

Complex people are generally busy people, but busy people get things done. I met this very complex person, Prophetess Cynthia Thompson, in a very relaxed posture. We were getting our hair done. Very uncomplicated, don't you think? The most striking thing was neither of us was in a conventional salon. We were in a hotel suite during a conference being pampered by the same professional stylist and becoming enraptured in the phenomenon of who each of us was then, and who we were about to become.

An unorthodox meeting has led to a very unorthodox relationship. I have watched her grow into an international prophetic voice with schools, a church (alongside her husband Billy Thompson), entrepreneurship, writer, author and mother to both natural and spiritual children. Eternal Change Ministries is transforming and changing lives worldwide because of that spark of unconventional, extraordinary spirit of the mother of its invention. If you want sameness, uninventive, church as usual, don't bother to call or come. If you want inventiveness, vivaciousness, beauty and sheer powerful prophetic, life impacting ministry, get into a meeting, a school session or a church service, and become enveloped into the culture of prophetic life. Come expecting a true encounter of "Eternal Change" and become lost in prophetic truth through books and instruction that take you to another realm of inventiveness.

Apostle Pam Vinnett
Author, Speaker and Founder of Pam Vinnett Ministries,
AIIM Institute and Fellowship

There is a growing trend to know the supernatural and that has produced an unhealthy appetite for the wrong things in this generation and culture of life. There is a strong desire in this generation to see and experience an unholy demonstration of the supernatural. Witchcraft is at an all time high in young children and teenagers. The psychic industry is a billion dollar marketplace because of the desire to know the future and what is going to happen in the lives of people.

With this being said, the church is in a unique position to demonstrate, teach, train and equip this generation for the supernatural. There is no better way to do that than through the apostolic and prophetic offices. They are the custodians of the supernatural for the church. These offices keep the focus on hearing God in the now, by responding to what the spirit is saying. Prophets interpret the signs of the times.

By purchasing this resource 'Power of a Prophetic Mindset, you will awaken your spiritual senses to the things of the spirit, and learn how to operate the prophetic. As Cynthia expresses in her book- "...I have simplified the prophetic to the following "the prophetic is the mind of God it is the power of the spiritual and supernatural coming together to invade the earth."

As a dear friend of Cynthia for over twenty years this is a long awaited book that has taken a lifetime of experience and wisdom to develop the vocabulary to make this practical for all who will value the calling to read it.

Dr. Renny McLean
Founder of Renny McLean Ministries, Texas

The prophetic has already been a much needed ministry in the church. Much needed but unfortunately misunderstood. Prophet Cynthia Thompson not only brings understanding of the gift but the office of the prophet. Therefore this is a must read for not only those that flow in the gift but stand in the office of the prophet.

Apostle E.G. Brinson
Apostolic Covering for Redeeming Word Christian Centers International

Prophetess Cynthia is a power house for God and a prophetic voice to nations. A national inspiration to the body of Christ. One who has stood on the cutting edge of prophetic significance for over two decades. She is the embodiment of the love of God for all people.

Prophetess Francina Norman
Francina Norman Ministries

It has been my privilege to have known and associated with Prophet Cynthia Thompson. As an International Director, I have seen the lack of true prophetic voices in the nations of the world. With the world crying out for direction, certainty and demonstration the church has been insufficient in providing that clear prophetic sound of this era.

This insufficiency in our world has created a spiritual vulnerability and opens the door for the false to flourish. These false messengers are highly skilled in their spiritual verbiage and tutorage. The result of this long and painful journey leads to captivity through their ways of communication. The promise of "cutting-edge" material and "breakthrough" initiatives leads one to doubt, fear and the inability for true freedom.

God hearing this plea has historically raised up the genuine voice of His concerns and direction. Prophet Cynthia is one of those voices in this hour. Her sensitivity to the voice and word of God qualifies her to send forth a sound into the earth today.

Prophet Cynthia has proven her loyalty, dedication, and devotion in the following areas: First of all, in her relationship with Jesus Christ. Secondly, with her zeal and continued witness to the Body of Christ and the surrounding world. Lastly, she is a faithful wife, friend, co-laborer and community leader.

It has been my privilege to serve with Prophet Cynthia in various venues. Her heart to share a positive, wholesome and prophetic lifestyle around the world has been an encouragement to many men and women. Prophet Cynthia has the evident characteristics of a woman with a call from God on her life; she demonstrates Godly character and principles, effective communication, and maturity of a leader.

The materials released from this woman of God are of the highest standard and can be enjoyed and will help anyone develop in their journey with God. It is with great honor and delight that I place my signature to her work and materials.

Dr. Terry L. Thompson
International Director

Foreword

In a day and time where the church is being called on more and more to bring insight, wisdom, knowledge and revelation; God sets some to share and prophesy His Word as we prepare for the second coming of our Lord. Prophet Cynthia has been anointed by God to take this generation into its next level of prophetic understanding. As enlightenment is manifested, men and women of spiritual discernment help us to see having yet seen.

As you read this book, let there be LIGHT in your life as you allow God's love to flow through you, with eyes and ears of understanding. I believe this book will help you stay in courage and will effectively motivate you as you allow the Holy Spirit to keep you on top of your charge.

As you get filled with the Words spoken through this prolific seer Prophet Cynthia Thompson, you will see yourself on the other side of these Words. You will see yourself, sharing, speaking, preaching, teaching and declaring. And just as John accounts the Words Jesus spoke to his disciples in the book of John chapter seven, "Out of your belly will flow, rivers of living water!"

To God be the Glory for raising my spiritual daughter, this powerful Prophet for such a time as this. I know her father, the late Bishop Isaiah S. Williams, Jr., would be so Godly proud! The publication of this book is a sign of God's timing to bring great victory, wisdom and revelation to those that read and receive.

In the bonds of peace, hope and love,

Shalom,

Dr. Gloria Y. Williams
Jesus People Ministries Church Inc.

Dedication

This book is dedicated to two of the most influential men in my life.

In memory of my spiritual father, the late Bishop Isaiah S. Williams Jr. founder of Jesus People Ministries Church International in Miami, Florida, who introduced me to the prophetic. I can remember the first day I came to the church I was broken, confused and without hope. His Words of love and unwavering position of righteousness gave me the courage to leave a life of celebrity, fame, and fortune to step into a new life filled with faith and love.

My first encounter with the supernatural realm of power came through him. He demonstrated the prophetic with signs and wonders following his ministry. I appreciated the many teachings on kingdom living, how to love my family and how to be faithful to God. He also taught me how to become grounded in the Word of God and to live a faith-focused life. Finally, I learned how to have an excellent spirit in all that I do. These teachings were the springboard for me to walk upright and in integrity regardless of circumstances.

As a daughter, I couldn't have asked for a better Father. A man of humor, honesty, integrity, impeccable character and most importantly full the Holy Ghost. Thank you for being a protector, provider and friend. I will never forget you as long as I live. Sir, you have left a mark that will never be erased.

To My Champion, William Stansberry Thompson Sr. A champion is a warrior, someone who fights for or defends a cause. He is unbeaten, undefeated and a world-class leader. You have proven to be a champion on the basketball court as well as God's court. I have seen many hits come your way to take you down but like a champion you always rise.

Thank you seems to be such an inadequate word to describe my appreciation for you. You are an incredible companion, lover and my best friend. You are God's perfect match for me because you love me with such tenderness and understand all of my complexities. You have enhanced my life and made me a better person.

Honey, thanks for believing in me, and allowing me to walk in my anointing without competition or strife. I honor you as my Pastor and as the priest of our home I admire your love for the Lord and for being sensitive to the Spirit of God in leading His people. You are the world's best father and "pa pa" because you patiently care for our children and grandchildren. I thank God that He chose me to be the mother of your children as well as use my spiritual womb to help give birth to your kingdom purpose. We are in this together and until Jesus comes… I look forward to standing as your prophetic partner to raise a generation for prophetic purpose.

My love for you is eternal!!!!!

Thank You

To My Father God, who has always been there for me, I don't have a vocabulary extensive enough to express how great you are. My Honor and respect for you Sir is beyond measure. You continue to prove your faithfulness towards me. Thank you for choosing me from my mother's womb to be a prophet for you and for entrusting me with your revelation. I count it an honor to impart your truth into the lives of many. I am committed to serving you for the rest of my days.

To my children Geneva, Arnell, Mercedes, Billy Jr, and Micaiah. I love you all so Much! Thank you for allowing me to be God spokesperson in the earth. You have shared me with so many people throughout your lives and I thank you for the unselfish love you guys always have demonstrated to others. Besides God, you all are the motivation and strength that gives me courage to continue leading a path for
others to follow.

To Courtney Beacham, my spiritual daughter, my adjutant, sounding board, trusted companion and friend. Only God could have sent you into my life, you are my extended brain, my encourager, defender, and counsel. Words can't express how much you mean to me, I don't have enough money in the earth (yet):-) to pay you for what you're worth. My prayer for you is that you never lack anything or want for nothing and that the Lord will satisfy the deep longings in your heart and fill you with long life. My you receive the double portion like Elisha who served Elijah. I love you

To my prophetic company thank you for your support, prayers and your faithfulness to God. For taking the leap and hanging in there with me through the tough assignments and late night prayer calls! Thank you for helping me birth this out. This is for us!! I Love you guys...

To my JPPIC family for all your prayers, the words of encouragement for every hug and token of love you continually show. Thank you for your prophetic hunger and willingness to obey God.....I love you all so much and I pray that this book take you to your next dimension.

A special thank you to Vanetta Gay and Sameko Munroe for hanging with me in the early morning hours to get this project finished, my writing crew who took my prayer life to another level lol!! All my extended family and close friends you guys are the real!!!!

Introduction

Most people automatically relegate the prophetic to the church or to the prophet and prophetic ministry, but the prophetic has been in existence since the foundation of the worlds. Contrary to popular belief, the prophetic is not just prophecy; it is the ministry of spiritual interpretation and it involves everyone who is willing to shift and tap into accessing God's mind. God instituted the prophetic so that we could understand how his mindset and his supernatural systems operate. While many people have written on the subject, it still remains mysterious to the masses.

The prophetic is the mind of God, which is available to everyone. It is not some mystical, spooky place that is only reserved for a select few. In fact, God wants everyone to know the prophetic, because it is how he operates in people, places and things to accomplish His will in the earth.

> **In the first chapter of the book of Genesis, God began to speak things into existence by saying, "Let there be" and whatever He spoke came into existence.**

As a teacher of the prophetic, I am on a mission to disseminate information and provide spiritual intelligence to demystify this powerful realm. Understanding the prophetic will teach you how to unlock your destiny– relationally, professionally, naturally, and spiritually – in every area of your life. In the first chapter of the book of Genesis, God began to speak things into existence by saying, "Let there be" and whatever he spoke came into existence.

The prophetic is so powerful, because it represents God speaking forth His thoughts outside of time to cause creation to respond in time to His original plan for mankind. In this book, you will not only learn about how the human mind works in contrast to the prophetic mind, but also how to utilize the prophetic because it is eternally tied to everything you will do.

My heart in writing this book is to simply offer my revelation and insight into the power gained from having a prophetic mindset. Prophetic people come in many types: some are lawyers, doctors, accountants, teachers, marketplace business leaders, psalmists, pastors, evangelists, prophets, seers, dreamer of dreams, and the list goes on. Abandon your fears and preconceived notions about the prophetic and take a journey with me to become empowered by this amazing resource God has given us to dominate in the earth realm.

The Power of a Prophetic Mindset is a road map that will equip you with strategies and tools to become successful. When you get God's mind, you will have a prophetic mind; when you have a prophetic mind, you will have power. Get ready to become the game-changer and global influencer who operates in supernatural power and authority!

CHAPTER 1

THE HUMAN MIND

For to be carnally minded is death; but to be spiritually minded is life and peace. Because the carnal mind is enmity against God: for it is not subject to the law of God, neither indeed can be.
Romans 8:6-7 KJV

KEY TERMS

Conscious [1] - awake and able to understand what is happening around you

Unconscious [2] - not marked by conscious thought, sensation, or feeling

Subconscious [3] - existing in the part of the mind that a person is not aware of; existing in the mind but not consciously known or felt

In order to understand the importance of having a prophetic mindset, you need to examine the human mind to learn how powerful it is. In the scripture above, there are two types of minds; one leads to submission and life and the other leads to opposition and death. In examining the human mind, you will discover why it is so important to tap into God's mind, as opposed to the human mind which carries the experiences and baggage of your past.

> *Brothers and sisters, I do not consider myself yet to have taken hold of it. But one thing I do: Forgetting what is behind and straining toward what is ahead, I press on toward the goal to win the prize for which God has called me heavenward in Christ Jesus.* -- **Philippians 3:13-14 TNIV**

What is the Human Mind?

The human mind is the faculty of consciousness and thought that enables an individual to process feelings, old and new experiences and good and bad thoughts. The mind influences how we function and operate every day. There are three parts of the mind the conscious, subconscious, and unconscious; all of them work together to create our natural reality.

The Conscious Mind is what allows us to communicate through speaking, pictures, writing, thought, and even our physical movements. On the other hand, the subconscious mind is in charge of our recent memories, and is in continuous contact with the resources of the unconscious mind. The unconscious mind stores memories and past experiences - those that have been suppressed because of devastation or trauma, and those that have simply been consciously forgotten and are no longer relevant. It's from these memories and experiences that our beliefs, habits, and behaviors are formed.

When looking at the mind, it is important to analyze each component of it in order to understand how each part processes information and has shaped where you are right now. God desires for believers to live in abundance and not be limited in any way. He wants them to be healthy, wealthy and strong, just like him. The subsequent scripture reveals God's heart when he created us:

> *And God said, Let us make man in our image, after our likeness: and let them have dominion over the fish of the sea, and over the fowl of the air, and over the cattle, and over all the earth, and over every creeping thing that creepeth upon the earth. So God created man in his own image, in*

the image of God created he him; male and female created he them. And God blessed them, and God said unto them, Be fruitful, and multiply, and replenish the earth, and subdue it: and have dominion over the fish of the sea, and over the fowl of the air, and over every living thing that moveth upon the earth. -- **Genesis 1:26-28 KJV**

> **We were created in the image of God which means within our DNA there is a supernatural ability to win and overcome!**

From the beginning of time, his plan was for us to have dominion-which is to dominate and rule-and to control circumstances in the earth as opposed to them ruling over or controlling us. We were created in the image of God which means within our DNA there is a supernatural ability to win and overcome! With this in mind, let's go a little deeper into the conscious part of the mind.

The Conscious Mind

The conscious mind directs your ability to focus and whatever you focus on, you will eventually become. There is an amazing connection between the heart and mind. The Word of God asserts "For as a man thinketh in his heart so is he." The human mind is limited to the earth realm. What the human mind produces is what you have already seen or experienced. It also deals with our imaginations which are not real. If you believe or focus on negative things, or reports of the world, then your subconscious will obediently deliver the feelings, emotions, and memories that you have associated with that type of thinking. And, because those feelings will become your reality, you can get caught up in a never-ending loop of negativity, fear, and anxiety, constantly looking for the bad in every situation.

For example, you go to the doctor and he gives you a diagnosis of a serious illness. You immediately get anxious and think the worst because your mind is conditioned to believe that negativity is absolute and real. The job of the conscious mind- where you do your thinking and logical reasoning- is to process the information at face value, and this is why you live your life in fear. On the other hand, when you have a prophetic mindset, you immediately access the spiritual and supernatural resources of heaven to prophesy and to make decrees and declarations according to the Word of God. Utilizing your prophetic resources will empower you to overturn everything contrary to the Word of God.

"What you decide on will be done, and light will shine on your ways."
-- Job 22:28 NLT

The Subconscious Mind

The second part of the mind is the subconscious, which plays an important role in our day-to-day functioning. It works hard, ensuring you have everything you need for quick recall and access when you need it. For example, things like your memory (how to ride a bike without consciously thinking about it), filters (your beliefs and values), sensations (the 5 senses) behaviors, habits and moods.

The subconscious is where psychologists say the "sixth sense" comes from. The "sixth sense" gives people the ability to perceive the unseen world. It also includes the ability to understand the cause-and-effect relationship behind many events, beyond the understanding of the human intellect. Other terms used for the "sixth sense" are Extrasensory Perception (ESP), clairvoyance, premonition, and intuition. These terms are synonymous with sixth sense, or subtle perception ability. [4] Science-through the intellect of the human mind-recognizes the "sixth sense", but we as believers recognize it as the prophetic. Believers don't operate with a sixth

THE HUMAN MIND

sense we operate prophetically. By this I mean that we, by way of the gifts of the spirit, can know things in advance and discern matters that the mind could never comprehend. This is why, as I will discuss in a later chapter, our minds must be transformed to think prophetically so that we can be on the cutting-edge of whatever we do.

The Unconscious Mind

> **Understanding the human mind and how it functions is essential to getting to the core of our thinking and belief system.**

The unconscious mind is very similar to the subconscious mind in that it also deals with our memories. The difference between the two is that the unconscious mind stores deep seated emotions that have been programmed in us since birth. If you desire to see an uprooting of things it is here-in the unconscious mind-that change must take place. Unconscious is the term that psychologists and psychiatrists use to refer to the thoughts that are "out of the reach" of our consciousness. In simple terms, the unconscious can be likened unto a vault where all memories that have been repressed- or those we don't wish to recall- are stored. A traumatic event in our childhood that has been blocked out is a good example. If we don't properly process out psychologically painful memories and submit every part of our minds to the power of God, we will find ourselves stuck; influenced by the past instead of the incredible future that God has ordained.

Understanding the human mind and how it functions is essential to getting to the core of our thinking and belief systems. Therefore, uprooting the deep-seated things that it has produced is critical in developing a prophetic disposition. The mind understands that all things are possible and that power and dominion belong to you. Within your DNA, God encoded his eternal thoughts because you were created in his likeness and image. Every limitation is broken when you operate with a prophetic mindset because you see things from Heaven's perspective, which is the mind of God. I challenge you to elevate your mind and spirit and shift from operating within the limitations of the human mind into the power of the prophetic mind. This change will make it easy to obey God when he positions us for our next move or even when ministering to his people. Remember, a prophetic attitude, will always give you an advantage in your career, business, relationships, at home, and all things pertaining your very existence, for it is an elevated way of reflecting and subsisting. Having an attitude of such permits you to always be on top.

CHAPTER 2

TRANSFORMATION OF THE MIND

Do not conform to the pattern of this world, but be transformed by the renewing of your mind. Then you will be able to test and approve what God's will is—his good, pleasing and perfect will.
Romans 12:2 NIV

KEY TERMS

Metamorphosis [5] - a major change in the appearance or character of someone or something

Wrestling [6] - to struggle to move, deal with, or control something

Let's establish this one most important thing from the very start: transformation in and of itself means to change completely, which means that whatever the thing is that is being changed has done so to the point of being totally reconfigured and looks nothing like it looked before the metamorphosis occurred. So, in order to transform the mind, there must be a dramatic change in the way one thinks and acts, such that the individual is virtually a stranger to his family, friends, and foes. Not strange, but a stranger in that an obvious change has taken place. I'd say

THE POWER OF A PROPHETIC MINDSET

that the whole transformational process could be compared to a wrestling match. Envision this: when two wrestlers get into a ring their whole objective is to "engage one another in an attempt to gain control, by using techniques designed to throw their opponents off balance and take them to the ground where they can achieve a dominant position. The objective is to pin down or subdue the opponent causing him to surrender to the greater power of the skill of the other." This utilization of techniques to gain control . . . causing one to surrender, is exactly what must happen with the mind in order to cultivate a prophetic mindset.

When the mind is transformed your very character and nature take on a new identity. God knew we could never fully represent him without a renewed mind because the way we think affects the way things are done.

> *For whom he did foreknow, he also did predestinate to be conformed to the image of his Son, that he might be the firstborn among many brethren.*
> -- **Romans 8:29 KJV**

God rules the heavens and he put us here to rule the earth, the only problem with this, is that we cannot rule with a mind that does not think God's thoughts. The Lord desires for us to look and act like him in the earth, not just when we get to heaven. When God created us he knew that we would be born in a world of twisted minds and fallen natures - an atmosphere filled with sin. What is so awesome about God is that he peered through time and eternity, preordering a "mind renewal" so we could think like him. The Lord desires for us to look like him and act like him in the earth, not just when we get to heaven. God rules the heavens and he put us here to rule the earth, the only problem with this, is that we cannot rule with a mind that does not think God's thoughts.

Fighting has been viewed as a negative thing, when in actuality the word fight itself is a verb — it's an action word. It requires you to act —

TRANSFORMATION OF THE MIND

> **When the mind is transformed your very character and nature takes on a new identity.**

not necessarily in a negative way — especially if you're moving towards an outcome that's good. What we've learned in America is that we have every right to fight for what we believe to be true. Whenever you take a stand against anything that is opposite of what you believe, it will meet you with resistance. This is why we wrestle because the opposing thing doesn't want to give in. As believer's we are fighting our way back to the original place we had with God so we can hear what we originally heard and knew from God. Satan does not want this to happen because, once you discover the power and influence you have been given over all the circumstances in your life with one word from God, Satan is in trouble. He can no longer hold you captive because of the sound of truth that emanates from a transformed mind.

Like wrestling, taking down the opposition - in essence the thoughts in your head - may require you to slam them down a few times before they are rendered defeated and ineffective to contend with you any longer. You must, then, be determined and resolute about wanting - and getting - the victory over this thing that has for too long controlled the direction in which your life is traveling. So, transforming your mind is not going to be something that is "won and done", it is, however, going to demand that you fight with everything in you to tear down notions and ideas that have reigned supreme in your life for generations, which will not be easy. But, the fight will certainly be worth it because God wants you mentally restructured, and that starts by making a concentrated effort to tear down images that are against God's thoughts for your life.

Daily, we must wrestle with the thoughts that run through our own minds. And, whether or not those thoughts elevate us to high places of victory and strength in God, or bring us down to some of the lowest, places possible in our flesh, we must take down those thoughts in order to tap into the mind of God concerning every area of our lives. Because the bottom line is it does not matter if the thoughts are the

> *Transformation is a wrestling process.*

greatest or the worst, if they are not in line with the Word of God, they still bring us to dry, desolate places in our lives.

> "Casting down imaginations, and every high thing that exalts itself against the knowledge of God, and bringing into captivity every thought to the obedience of Christ." -- **2 Corinthians 10:5 KJV**

This passage of scripture says it best, because the phrase "casting down" literally means to take down with the use of force; to pull down; demolish the subtle reasonings (of opponents) likened to a fortress. And, this is why I say that transformation is a wrestling process. In order for you to hear and do what you knew to originally (naturally) hear and do, you must fight your way back to the original plan of God, which is what you originally knew. If you do not fight to hear and do what God has said, believe me when I tell you someone, somewhere is waiting to tell you what they want you to hear and do. You are probably thinking I'm just talking, but I am not. Adam and Eve, if they could, would testify to the importance of slamming down and "bringing into captivity every thought to the obedience of Christ."

Obedience is Essential to Transformation

God intends to "do us good and make us happy." If you recall the story of Adam and Eve, God placed them in the Garden of Eden which is a beautiful place that had everything they would ever need. The word Eden in Hebrew means "delight" or "enjoyment"—it was a garden of delight or enjoyment and some translators have associated the word paradise with it. Spiritually, Eden symbolizes a rich and fertile place of unbroken fellowship.

In this place, we see where the first wrestling match began between Satan and Adam and Eve.

> Now the serpent was more subtil than any beast of the field which the LORD God had made. And he said unto the woman, Yea, hath God said, Ye shall not eat of every tree of the garden? And the woman said unto the serpent, We may eat of the fruit of the trees of the garden: But of the fruit of the tree which is in the midst of the garden, God hath said, Ye shall not eat of it, neither shall ye touch it, lest ye die . And the serpent said unto the woman, Ye shall not surely die: For God doth know that in the day ye eat thereof, then your eyes shall be opened , and ye shall be as gods, knowing good and evil. And when the woman saw that the tree was good for food, and that it was pleasant to the eyes, and a tree to be desired to make one wise , she took of the fruit thereof, and did eat , and gave also unto her husband with her; and he did eat. And the eyes of them both were opened, and they knew that they were naked; and they sewed fig leaves together, and made themselves aprons. And they heard the voice of the LORD God walking in the garden in the cool of the day: and Adam and his wife hid themselves from the presence of the LORD God amongst the trees of the garden. And the LORD God called unto Adam, and said unto him, where art thou? And he said, I heard thy voice in the garden, and I was afraid, because I was naked; and I hid myself. And he said, Who told thee that thou wast naked? Hast thou eaten of the tree, whereof I commanded thee that thou shouldest not eat?
>
> **-- Genesis 3:1-11 KJV**

Here, we see that God gave them specific instructions not to eat from the tree in the middle of the garden. Satan presented to them a different thought than God's. Satan asked them if God had forbidden them from eating from every tree of the garden – getting them to question what they already knew was the truth! And, instead of them forcefully throwing those thoughts down to the ground, and fighting to obey what God said, Adam and Eve started chewing on (meditating), then swallowing what the devil

> *Disobedience is one of the main opponents you will have to wrestle and take down in order a have a prophetic mindset.*

said. Subsequently, Adam and Eve allowed their minds to be free, instead of bringing into captivity those thoughts that were disobedient to God's mind. Once they bit the fruit, we see the lie - which is sin - begin to contend with the righteous thoughts of God. We don't know how many opportunities Eve had to wrestle with the conversations she had with Satan before he won the fight; but we do know he strategically gained control of this match, and the rest is history. We see the outcome of his victory over them; the fruit of disobedience was birthed into the earth. Once this took place, Adam and Eve no longer had access to the realm of revelation, and it was then that a spiritual separation between God and them took place. This is the reason why you and I must now boldly fight to win this last round of transformation by a Total Knock Out!

When Adam and Eve ate of the tree of the knowledge of good and evil, it was at that moment that the thoughts and mind of a lower world were birthed into mankind. This is the point when "sin thoughts" showed up in the minds of Adam and Eve and God had to separate his thoughts from those of sin. Most professional wrestling matches are fixed fights, which means they know what the end (win, lose, draw) is going to be before the battle even begins – just like God knew about you . . . us. God predestined and designed us to win from the foundation of the worlds! Disobedience is one of the main opponents you will have to wrestle and take down in order a have a prophetic mindset. In every situation God presents, we have choices, and if we choose obedience our lives will be transformed forever.

TRANSFORMATION OF THE MIND

The Mind of the Flesh vs. The Mind of the Spirit

Now the mind of the flesh (which is sense and reason without the Holy Spirit) is death (death that comprises all miseries arising from sin, both here and hereafter.) but the mind of the (holy) spirit is life and (soul) peace (both now and forever.) -- **Romans 8:6 Amplified**

There is a mindset that will always block the flow of the prophetic and this is the mind of the flesh. A carnal or fleshly way of thinking will always be at odds with the prophetic mindset because, a prophetic mindset gives you instant access to the past, present and future.

> ***A carnal or fleshly mindset will always be at odds with the prophetic mindset.***

Whether you are currently in ministry, own a business or you work on a corporate job, the prophetic mind gives you the favored position over others because you can access information and strategies to be "the head and not the tail." For too long, the mind of the flesh has governed the decisions we make and we can no longer be ruled by this lower nature. We will never be able to walk in kingdom, power, ruler ship and authority to defeat the enemy with the mind of the flesh. The mind of the flesh is a carnal mind and Romans 8:6 clearly talks about the perils of operating in this mentality.

The mind of the flesh-which largely deals with the cravings and desires of what we want and not what God desires-, is what we were taught and trained to focus on and believe in, it is a mind of reason and sense. As a result, anything that does not make sense [we can't see, hear, touch, taste or smell] or we can't reason with because of our fleshly minds we dismiss it as senseless. The irony of it all is that what we deem as crazy is often God wanting to stretch us to new levels of faith, instead of having us rely on reason and senses, which is "fallen faith."

THE POWER OF A PROPHETIC MINDSET

Our lives in Christ should be spirit-led life. The sole purpose of the mind of the flesh leads you to death and opposes whatever God stands for. As a young believer I learned very early that I couldn't live a successful spirit-led life and follow the behaviors and habits that were etched in my mind prior to salvation. The Apostle Paul helps us to see the spiritual battle between the spirit and the flesh, in the following passage of scripture:

> *So I find it to be a law (rule of action of my being) that when I want to do what is right and good, evil is ever present with me and I am subject to its insistent demands. For I endorse and delight in the Law of God in my inmost self [with my new nature]. But I discern in my bodily members in the sensitive appetites and wills of the flesh] a different law (rule of action) at war against the law of my mind (my reason) and making me a prisoner to the law of sin that dwells in my bodily organs [in the sensitive appetites and wills of the flesh].*
> **-- Romans 7:21-23 Amplified**

The battle between the flesh and the spirit rages because the flesh doesn't want you to submit to the Spirit of Christ. As you develop and cultivate a prophetic mindset, the Spirit of Christ will cause you to embrace greatness. Norman Vincent Peele, a great Christian motivational speaker, once said, "Change your thoughts and you change your world." The mind of the spirit-the prophetic mind - will produce thoughts that will help you to change your life and ultimately your world.

CHAPTER 3

UNDERSTANDING THE PROPHETIC

We also have the prophetic message as something completely reliable, and you will do well to pay attention to it, as to a light shining in a dark place, until the day dawns and the morning star rises in your hearts.
2 Peter 1:19 NIV

KEY TERMS

Realm [7] - A range or field of control, power, or other concentration of mastery and or authority.

Power [8] - to give impetus to; to move with great speed or force

According to T. Austin Sparks (1954), author of Prophetic Ministry, the prophetic is the mind of God. It is the ministry voice that interprets the mind of God to his people. It is the ministry of spiritual interpretation.[9] I am an Apostolic Prophet and whenever I talk about the prophetic many people both outside and inside of the church automatically think I am referring to prophecy. The prophetic is so much bigger than prophecy and goes beyond telling someone their name (which they should already know), that they will get married, become wealthy or move to a new home. The medium of prophecy gives you information; however, the prophetic tears down, establishes, builds, charges, ignites, navigates, re-directs and steers. So with this being said, I have simplified the definition to the following: "the prophetic is the power of the spiritual and supernatural coming together to invade the earth."

> *The prophetic and the prophet's mantle hasn't been fully embraced because there hasn't been clear understanding of the role and function of prophetic ministry.*

For years, we have been taught many different things concerning the prophetic and the prophet's office. The prophetic and the prophet's mantle have not been fully embraced because a clearer understanding of the role and function of prophetic ministry needs to be established. Ironically, the greatest opposition to the prophetic has come from pastors. Perhaps fear, along with their desire to protect their flocks from unseasoned and uneducated prophets, caused them to establish tight boundaries to restrict the ministry of the prophetic in the churches. While understandable, the enemy took full advantage of the fear of leaders by shutting out prophetic voices. As a result, we began to see pastors focus more on winning souls and becoming evangelical, as opposed to forming Christ within the souls of the saints through the prophetic.

Over the last 25+ years, we saw the number of believers grow each year and mega-churches sprang up in cities across America and all over the world. I am not against church growth, in fact Acts 2:47 says "...And the Lord added to the church daily..." Church growth is wonderful; however, increasing numbers without increasing spiritual knowledge is counterproductive.

The absence of the prophetic from the church has caused us to see kids turn to drugs, gang violence, dark occultic realms-like Harry Potter, The

Twilight series, werewolves and vampires. Further, issues of divorce, same sex marriages, perversion, abortion, and leadership burnout began to run rampant and manifest in the church. So now the place that once housed the power, to ward-off attacks and defend the hurting, has become weakened because there is no prophetic guard in our churches to protect the Body of Christ. Since the prophetic has been shut out, the enemy has beens successful at doing his job, as his mission was to remove the eyes from the Body. Naturally, eyes help you to see which way to go but when the prophetic is silenced, it will be difficult to hear the thoughts of God. This is where knowledge of the prophetic steps in to offer strategies and solutions.

> **The prophetic is the greatest establishment in the earth because it represents the mind of God.**

The prophetic is not some mystical, spooky place that is only reserved for a select few. It is in fact, the greatest establishment in the earth because it causes the invisible to become visible. God wants everyone to have knowledge about how the prophetic functions, operates, speaks, and manifests. The prophetic is the power source God used to create the world and every living thing he placed in it. An example of this is found in the first chapter of the book of Genesis where God began to speak things into existence by saying, "Let there be" and the things He spoke came into being. Think about that for a moment; God has an agency in which he utilizes spiritual and natural agents to accomplish his will and that agency is the prophetic.

I love the spiritual and supernatural realms, just like I love sci-fi, superheroes and movies where the characters do unusual and extraordinary things because they remind me of the prophetic and

THE POWER OF A PROPHETIC MINDSET

> *The prophetic is the power of the spiritual and supernatural coming together to invade the earth.*

supernatural occurrences. Operating in prophetic realms can be likened unto having "superhero" abilities. To me, Jesus Christ is the original superhero from which all others were modeled. He did extraordinarily profound miracles, like walk on water, raise the dead, turn water into wine and heal the sick before there was ever a thought about Superman, Captain America or even the Hulk. So, when I affirm my love for science fiction and superheroes they remind me of Jesus who is the greatest hero of them all!

The prophetic realms are available for everyone. Most people shy away from learning more about the prophetic because they feel that it is reserved for those called into full time-ministry or more specifically into the office of the prophet. You are more prophetic than you realize. If you dream, have visions, experience déjà vu, get a "gut" feeling about something that is about to happen and it actually happens or you may know things about a person you've never met before then you are prophetic. In this season, people are having spiritual and supernatural encounters like never before.

> *And it shall come to pass afterward, that I will pour out my spirit upon all flesh; and your sons and your daughters shall prophesy, your old men shall dream dreams, your young men shall see visions.*
> -- Joel 2:28 KJV

This scripture shows us that dormant potential of the prophetic resides in everyone and that God's heart is for everyone to operate prophetically.

UNDERSTANDING THE PROPHETIC

Prophetic Resources

You may be asking, "How do I operate prophetically?" In order to operate prophetically, you have to know the many resources that are contained within the prophetic. The prophetic houses the following spiritual tools:

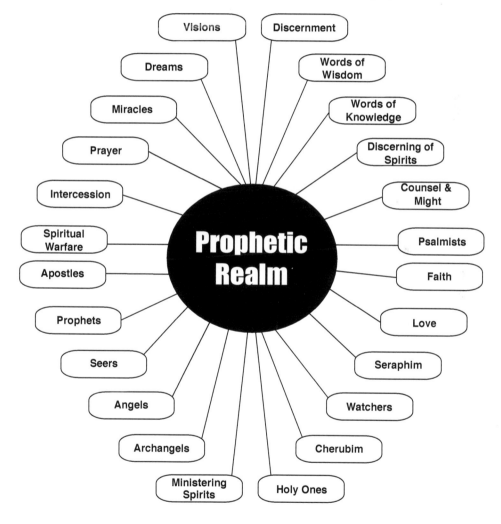

Some of the tools don't require any effort on your part; however, others require you to pray, declare or perform an action to activate the power of the resource.

The Force of the Prophetic

The prophetic has a vast backing to support the power contained within its realm. When you really look at the list above, you can rejoice knowing that there is a force available for back-up and support. "For I know the thoughts that I think toward you, saith the LORD, thoughts of peace, and not of evil, to give you an expected end." (Jeremiah 29:11). The prophetic force is mighty so going forward, enlist the prophetic force to go to war on your behalf.

The fivefold was given to build and equip the Body by utilizing all five officers. We may all have different gifts, classifications, spheres of influence and measures of rule but it is important to remember they all have been given for one purpose and that is to fortify the kingdom. Jesus said it best in Mark 9:39-40: "Do not restrain or hinder or forbid him, for no one who does a mighty work in My name will soon afterward be able to speak evil of Me. For he who is not against us is for us."

Now more than ever, we must work overtime to put in place-through prophetic schools and institutions, trainings and seminars - apostolic structures to help the evangelical minded church learn the prophetic and be able to receive and utilize the prophetic ministry.

God is calling us forth to merge our mantles and work together as governmental forces with spiritual intelligence to demonstrate the power of his kingdom and to become his hands extended in the earth. Remember, the prophetic is not just prophecy; it is the ministry of spiritual interpretation and supernatural power.

CHAPTER 4

CULTIVATING A PROPHETIC MINDSET

For as a man thinks in his heart so is he, not as he thinks in his head.
Proverbs 23:7 Amplified

KEY TERMS

Cultivation [10] - knowing that something exists or is happening

Mindset [11] - not marked by conscious thought, sensation, or feeling

In order to benefit from the prophetic, you must be willing to change the way you think and open your heart and mind to receive truth about this powerful supernatural realm. The heart is the cultivating ground of change however; it is the mind where all decisions are made.

Let me explain; the heart houses your mind, will and emotions, and it holds the greatest influence to every decision in life. This is why we have to guard the heart because out of it flows the issues of life. I often tell people we don't receive the things we ask of God because we are divided about what we are asking of God. Think about this: when most Christians pray,

THE POWER OF A PROPHETIC MINDSET

they ask God to do something that is their head; but, oftentimes their heart cries out for something totally different. This is the essence of being double-minded.

> [For being as he is] a man of two minds (hesitating, dubious, irresolute), [he is] unstable and unreliable and uncertain about everything [he thinks, feels, decides].
> -- **James 1:8 Amplified**

> *The heart is the cultivating ground of change however; it is the mind where all decisions are made.*

Our minds must become set in what God says. When we set something somewhere, we are placing it where we want it to be, locking it in a particular locality, or placing it in its proper position. We will need the mind of Christ if we are going to be effective in the ministry work of the kingdom. The process of renewing the mind involves uprooting old thoughts and replacing them with new thoughts. But, before we can put in new thoughts, the ground-of the mind- must be broken up and then cultivated. The cultivation process entails preparing the ground in a way that will promote optimal growth and development, especially through education and training. We live in an information-rich society where knowledge can be obtained by the click of a button. Ignorance is not bliss and we can't afford to continue to allow religion, fears, doctrines, evangelical minds and traditional views on the prophetic to keep the church from progressing and operating in its fullest power.

A prerequisite to having a prophetic mindset is tilling the soil of your mind. Tilling the soil of the mind involves picking, plucking, plowing up religious thoughts that may have caused you to be in a dry or even barren place in your salvation. If you are in a dry place right now, it is because you are lacking an intimate relationship with the Holy Spirit. Undoubtedly, this will cause you to feel like a dead man walking, but John 6:63 offers us hope because, *"The Spirit gives life; the flesh counts for nothing."*

The Holy Spirit + The Word of God = New Light

The Spirit represents the water which is the Word of God. Going forward, you must take The Word of God and put it in the soil of your newly prepared-for planting and growth-mind, so that new seeds of God-thoughts can grow. This will replace and root out old religious thoughts eternally. If you only get the word in seed- form and not the spirit of God that comes with the word-which is the water -you will never be able to come to full maturation and manifestation in the earth realm. If this happens, the earth begins to moan and groan because a seed has aborted its purpose. As a matter of fact, no seed whether natural or spiritual will grow without water-it will simply wither up and die because water is essential to life. Many Christians have good intentions, because they spend a lot of time reading the word but, the problem is that they never open their hearts to receive the spirit [which is water and the glory which is light.] Water and light are life sources for seeds causing them to grow.

Have you ever wondered why people who seem to be faithful church members receive good seed (Word), yet they don't seem to smile or have the fruits of joy or peace? The answer is simple: they have not allowed the Holy Spirit to cultivate fruit and relationship in their lives. The Holy Spirit is the water that helps you grow in the word that has been assigned in your life. His job is to lead you into the light of God's glory so you can be set free and grow.

The word is spirit and life and within the word there is water and light to produce life. When a farmer plants a seed, he expects to get from the seed what is in the seed. The same holds true with Jesus Christ. He expects you

THE POWER OF A PROPHETIC MINDSET

> **The word is spirit and life and within the Word there is water and light to produce life.**

to bear fruit based on the level of the word planted in you.

But the fruit of the spirit is love, joy, peace, long suffering, gentleness, goodness, faith, meekness, temperance: against such there is no law. **-- Galatians 5:22 KJV**

If you receive the Word of God into your heart and not just into your head, you will produce all of the fruit of the spirit. I love the parable of the sower. As you read this story, perhaps you will gain a better understanding of the process of letting the word cultivate your mind.

A sower went out to sow his seed: and as he sowed, some fell by the way side; and it was trodden down, and the fowls of the air devoured it. And some fell upon a rock; and as soon as it was sprung up, it withered away, because it lacked moisture. And some fell among thorns; and the thorns sprang up with it, and choked it. And other fell on good ground, and sprang up, and bare fruit an hundredfold. And when he had said these things, he cried, He that hath ears to hear, let him hear. And his disciples asked him, saying, What might this parable be? And he said, Unto you it is given to know the mysteries of the kingdom of God: but to others in parables; that seeing they might not see, and hearing they might not understand. Now the parable is this: The seed is the Word of God. Those by the way side are they that hear; then cometh the devil, and taketh away the Word out of their hearts, lest they should believe and be saved. They on the rock are they, which, when they hear, receive the Word with joy; and these have no root, which for a while believe, and in time of temptation fall away. And that which fell among thorns are they, which, when they have heard, go forth, and are choked with cares and riches and pleasures of this life, and bring no fruit to perfection. But that on the good ground are they, which in an honest and good heart, having heard the Word, keep it, and bring forth fruit with patience. **-- Luke 8:5-15 ESV**

I would like to paint a picture of this with Christ being the sower that gave his word to us as seed and we being the ground in which he scatters it. Some of us have been hardened by life's issues so we close our hearts to receiving the word. When the word falls by the wayside-it doesn't penetrate the heart- and is discarded. Others may only take the word at face value. If we keep it in our head and it never goes deep enough into the heart when the trials of life appear, it will be plucked out of the head and never reach the heart. Finally, there are those who take in the word and start to grow however, other things influence them so that eventually, the good seed of the Word of God is totally choked out. One of the greatest pleasures of the Father is when He sees us take in the seed and allow the water and light to nurture it so that we can grow and bear fruit.

My Process

The Holy Spirit is my best friend. I can remember when I rededicated my life to The Lord, I would stay up all night praying and talking to the Holy Spirit. I would ask questions about everything because I wanted more of him. Early in my walk, as a young Christian I used to ask God what happened to so many people in church, because I didn't see the fruit or evidence of their salvation. I wasn't being judgmental, but when I gave my life and my heart to the Lord, I was determined not to remain the same. I gave up a life of fame, fortune, fast cars and all that the world could offer. I was living high. Nothing was too good and no price tag was too expensive. I walked away from everything because I wanted to finally live a life filled with peace and joy. I questioned God because I didn't see real change, a love for God and transformation taking place in many people's lives after their confession of salvation. My life was taking on another shape, I was able to love and hug people who I thought were mean and unlovable. Joy flooded my heart and I knew that there was something strangely different going on in me. I discovered that my mind was being renewed and I was growing and producing fruit of the spirit called love. As I have grown, I

THE POWER OF A PROPHETIC MINDSET

realize that everyone is given the same seed from God but not everyone allows it to be planted in their hearts. I've learned that you must not only take the Word in your heart but you must drink of the water of the spirit and bask in the light of his glory and his presence to be changed. I've also learned that it's not the Word in your head that changes you; it's the word in your heart that brings change in you. My journey enabled me to identify five essential keys - prayer, transformation of the mind, death, studying the Word of God, Christ formed in you - to establishing and unlocking a prophetic mindset.

Key #1 Prayer

...The effective prayer of a righteous man can accomplish much. Elijah was a man with a nature like ours, and he prayed earnestly that it would not rain, and it did not rain on the earth for three years and six months. Then he prayed again, and the sky poured rain and the earth produced its fruit. **-- James 5:16-17 NASB**

Prayer connects you to God's way of thinking. It is a tool that allows us to communicate with God to get heaven to respond on our behalf. Whether we are in need of angelic backing, supernatural healing, witty ideas, strategies, financial increase and the like prayer is the weapon to get the job done.

Prayer is powerful and can change the course of nations, your destiny and the world. In I Kings 17:1 Elijah, one of the most profound prophets shows us the power of a prophetic mindset through prayer. In the

CULTIVATING A PROPHETIC MINDSET

aforementioned scripture, he gives a prophetic word to King Ahab stating "As the LORD, the God of Israel, lives, whom I serve, there will be neither dew nor rain in the next few years except at my Word." Elijah prayed for the rain not to fall for over three years and it did not fall. Imagine the impact of not having rain in Israel. He then prayed a prophetic prayer and the skies opened up again and rain fell on the land. Through prayer, Elijah was able to cause a drought to end to usher in an abundance of rain for the children of Israel.

THE POWER OF A PROPHETIC MINDSET

Transformation of the Mind

Do not be conformed to this world (this age), [fashioned after and adapted to its external, superficial customs], but be transformed (changed) by the [entire] renewal of your mind [by its new ideals and its new attitude], so that you may prove [for yourselves] what is the good and acceptable and perfect will of God, even the thing which is good and acceptable and perfect [in His sight for you]. **-- Romans 12:2 Amplified**

Renewing the mind is perhaps one of the most important keys to cultivating a prophetic mindset. The reason why it is of utmost importance is because the things-whether they be people, experiences or our education-that control our thinking ultimately become what directs and controls our lives. Basically, how we think affects how we feel and how we produce at work, ministry or play. How we feel, then, impacts our desires and how we dream or fail to reach for more in life. Our desires produce the actions which show the world whether or not we pray and believe what the Word of God says concerning us.

Moreover, if Satan controls our thinking by keeping us weighed down by our own natural, emotional way of responding, we are defeated because the prophetic will have no room to operate. A renewed mind believes what the word says and everything else becomes an "evil report" if it doesn't line up with the word. A prophetic mind will always war against the influences of Satan that try to prevent us from believing God to obtain his promises.

Further, Satan knows he wins whenever we are consumed with our own problems, our own trials and our own circumstances.

Without a doubt, this extinguishes the flame of God's Spirit in us, and as a result, none of his light or love will be able to shine forth. We'll be forced to "live a lie." We must always realize that every battle is a spiritual battle and the battle for our mind determines whether we sink or swim. Without a transformation of the mind, we can't operate with the Mind of Christ.

I want you to remember, in order to accomplish your desires or goals, there must be an "entire renewal of the mind." Although you may change your ideas, if your attitude doesn't change it will hinder the progress towards transformation. Transformation then is taking on an entire new and different form in your thought life.

Key #3 — Death

I assure you, most solemnly I tell you, unless a grain of wheat falls into the earth And dies, it remains(just one grain; becomes more but lives) by itself alone. But if it dies, it produces many others and yields a rich harvest.   **-- John 12:24 Amplified**

When a farmer goes out to plant a seed, he doesn't sit and hold the seed in his hand wondering what may come out of it. The farmer understands that if he doesn't put the seed in the ground, the potential that is within the seed will remain within it, and that potential will never be released for the benefit of others to enjoy. The seed must also be willing to yield itself to the soil, water and sun in order to bring forth the harvest that's in it. Love and concern in providing and taking care of others is the primary reason why the farmer plants. The parable of the sower is so powerful to help you discover this important key of death. Many times we see death as the end, but God sees death as the beginning. Love was introduced to the world by death. "God loved the world: He gave his son, his one and only son. and this is why: so that no one need be destroyed; by believing in him, anyone can have a whole and lasting life. (John 3:16 Message Bible)

Too often, we focus on the "doing in love" instead of "the dying in love." Once you grow into God's love which is Agape love it will be easy to deny yourself.

If any man will come after me let him deny himself and take up his cross and follow me. For who so ever will save his life shall lose it, and who so ever will lose his life for my sake shall find it. **-- Matthew 16:24-25 KJV**

Life in the spirit comes by way of self denial, the more you die to your selfish ways the more you will walk in the life of the spirit. The road of a disciple is death. Jesus could have never taken on the cross if he didn't have foreknowledge of the power that would come out of it. Once He conquered death it freed us to eternal living. When you discover that death has no power over you, there is nothing you can't accomplish. What many people fear the most is death, but out of death comes power! Power is not released to you until you have given all of yourself for it. When God sees that you are willing to give up all for Him, he will not withhold anything from you.

Studying the Word of God

Study and be eager and do your utmost to present yourself to God approved (tested by trial), a workman who has no cause to be ashamed, correctly analyzing and accurately dividing [rightly handling and skillfully teaching] the Word of Truth. -- **2 Timothy 2:15 Amplified**

We are living in an hour where Jesus is soon to return. We can look at all of the prophetic signs around which are dictating the closeness of his return. From the supernatural appearances of the four blood moons that will appear from April 2014 through October 2015, to the global conflicts involving Israel, Russia and other nations, the handwriting of the times is on the wall. The Sons of Issachar had a prophetic anointing which enabled them to be able to discern and know the times and seasons - have advance knowledge about what was coming ahead. We can see why this is crucial in I Timothy 4:1, "Now the Holy Spirit tells us clearly that in the last times some will turn away from the true faith; they will follow deceptive spirits and teachings that come from demons." Deception is deadly because it is designed to lead you away from the truth of God's word every time.

Studying the Word of God, not only validates you as an ambassador of God, but it empowers you to take on His character with boldness. T. Austin Sparks once said: "People come to see who you are more than to just hear what you have to say." This means that as you live the word there should be evidence of prosperity because abundant living comes by application and study of the word of God. It won't happen by studying the doctrines of men, or the opinions contained in commentaries but by the revelation which comes from studying the Bible. The Bible, which is our kingdom constitutional law book, outlines all of our rights and privileges as a kingdom citizens. Therefore, when studying the Bible you learn who you are and all the wonderful benefits that have been given. When you know these things you can represent our God proudly and never feel intimidated or ashamed.

Key #5 — Christ Formed In You

To whom God would make known what is the riches of the glory of this mystery among the Gentiles; which is Christ in you, the hope of glory:
-- Colossians 1:27 KJV

The issue of having Christ formed in believers has been an ongoing problem from the days of the Apostles to this current dispensation. There are three dispensations: the dispensation of the law, the dispensation of grace and the dispensation of the kingdom. Some of you may be asking why this is relevant and I am glad that inquiring minds want to know. In the dispensation of the law we were given rules because man's mind was not governed by God. When we don't house God's mind we are subject to sin and carnal thinking. In the dispensation of grace Jesus came to introduce us to His mind, meaning His way of thinking, and doing things. The dispensation of grace - is the prophetic mind of God **coming into the earth.** He didn't just introduce us to His mind he gave us the ability to live His mind so that Christ may be formed in us. The kingdom dispensation is the prophetic mind of God **ruling in the earth**. Kingdom causes us to rule with God's thoughts. The full manifestation of the kingdom operating in our lives is Christ being fully formed and embodied in us to manifest the glory.

Therefore, we can now see God's complete thought to have Christ formed in us because He **told us what to do** through the law, He **showed us what to do** through His grace and **empowers us to do** by His kingdom. Christ exhibited all of these things when He came to earth to demonstrate God's thought for us to live victoriously.

CHAPTER 5

A HIGHER WAY OF THINKING

For as the heavens are higher than the earth, so are my ways higher than your ways, and my thoughts than your thoughts.
Isaiah 55:9 ESV

KEY TERMS

Perspective [12] - The capacity to view things in their true relations or relative importance

Dispensation [13] - Administration

Shifting into a higher way of thinking requires you to not only be transformed in your mind, but for you to study and read the word and have a consistent prayer life. You might be saying: "I read the word and have a prayer life," but I'm talking about entering into a place where you can access revelation, and get it in its purest form.

Everyone has the privilege to get revelation by way of the spirit. When Jesus died the veil was rent. This is significant because the rending of the veil meant that Christ, by his death, opened a way-for all of us - to God.

THE POWER OF A PROPHETIC MINDSET

Therefore, he created a portal-an opening- for us to access the throne of grace, or mercy-seat.

> *And Jesus cried out again with a loud voice, and yielded up His spirit. And behold, the veil of the temple was torn in two from top to bottom; and the earth shook and the rocks were split.* -- **Matthew 27:50-51 NIV**

> **Revelation and transformation comes as a result of spending time with the Lord.**

> *Who shall ascend into the hill of The Lord? Or who shall stand in his holy place? He that hath clean hands, and a pure heart; who hath not lifted up his soul unto vanity, nor sworn deceitfully.* -- **Psalm 24:3-4 KJV**

There are requirements to go into the high places in God and living a clean-not perfect-lifestyle is important. The Holy Spirit gives us access into the supernatural, and thus, the prophetic realms. The Holy Spirit is like our GPS system which leads us directly into the high places of God, where His revelatory thoughts reside.

> **The Holy Spirit is like our GPS system which leads us directly into the high places of God, where His revelatory thoughts reside.**

Living a spirit-led life is critical in our relationship with God.

> *Which things we also speak, not in words taught by human wisdom, but in those taught by the Spirit, combining spiritual thoughts with spiritual words. But a natural man does not accept the things of the Spirit of God, for they are foolishness to him; and he cannot understand them, because they are spiritually appraised.* -- **I Corinthians 2:13-14 NASB**

A HIGHER WAY OF THINKING

A renewed mind is the precursor to lead you to a higher and better way of thinking by way of the Spirit, so that you can be powerful and defeat the enemy. Higher thoughts of the spirit mean that you will begin to walk in the perfect will of God.

> *And be constantly renewed in the spirit of your mind [having a fresh mental and spiritual attitude]* -- **Ephesians 4:23 Amplified**

Pnuema intelligence is the term for wisdom knowledge and insight of the spirit over the natural spheres of God's creation. It is meant to bring you into spiritual intelligence.

> *But God hath revealed them unto us by his Spirit: for the Spirit searcheth all things, yea, the deep things of God.* -- **I Corinthians 2:10 ISV**

> **Carnal thinking, which leads to reasoning and intellectualization, is a form of pride.**

One revelation or word from the Lord can change your whole life. The bible is replete with examples of how the Holy Spirit spoke things to people, or how the Lord employed the supernatural realm, either by the use of angels or dreams to impart revelation. No matter how intellectual you are, the natural man with the wisdom of the world, can't comprehend the things of the Spirit of God. Carnal thinking, which leads to reasoning and intellectualization, is a form of pride which opposes spiritual thinking or thoughts. We will never know the mind of God by natural power.

Seek Revelation Knowledge

Walking in the power of the prophetic is like living heaven on earth. Supernatural living and the advantage that the prophetic affords us, gives us the ability to overcome obstacles, download creative strategies and even receive witty ideas. Perhaps, you can see why the Lord said, " My thoughts are not your thoughts neither are my ways your ways, for as high as the heaven is above the earth so are my thoughts higher than yours." God's thoughts come out of the spirit and not of the earth.

Thoughts, impressions and ideas that come by way of revelation free us from bondage. Even though a higher way of thinking and accessing the mind of God is available, most believers tend to be lazy and choose to live by fallen information instead of revelation. Revelation and information can be likened to light and darkness. Revelation comes from the spirit which produces light and fallen information emanates from dark realms. I love the quote "Why settle for good when great is available." Fallen information is knowledge that already exists in the earth. Anything that already exists in the earth can ensnare you because it doesn't contain what is in the "now" of God.

The Dark Realm

Fallen information comes from familiar spirits. The term familiar spirit was derived from the generation spirit that supplied a family with its supernatural knowledge, worldly possessions and success, and spiritual wisdom. That spirit was thought to belong to the family line; therefore it was worshipped and sought for ancient and spiritual divine light and knowledge. Spiritism, necromancy, and psychic revelation were believed to come to certain "gifted" members of the family by this medium, which received his or her powers from the demons Satan assigned to the family line.[14]

Fallen spirits are incapable of accessing the realm of the living God. The function of these spirits is to download seed-thoughts and words filled with untruths and lies which cause believers to accept Satan's reports. The influence of Satan is great, and as we saw earlier, he was successful in interjecting a lower thought to Eve in the Garden of Eden to get her to eat from the tree of the knowledge of good and evil. Imagine that: Adam and Eve walked and talked with God every day. They had an up close and personal relationship with God and yet they were seduced by a fallen spirit. We are living in an hour where we can't afford to listen to, or be influenced by, any sound other than the Spirit of God.

Any thought or conversation, that may come from your family blood line, I don't care if it is your mother, father, sister, brother, grandmother etc., which seeks to get you to believe or repeat things that don't produce life or God thoughts, must be rejected! Family members are closest to you and can easily get you off course if you don't prophetically discern the spirits in which they operate (always remember Adam and Eve.) Some of us are living in bondage to sickness, working on dead-end jobs, experiencing debt, or even involved in bad relationships, because we've adopted a mentality of failure and defeat as a result of strong family soul ties. In summation, Colossians 2:8 says, *"Beware lest any man spoil you through philosophy and vain deceit, after traditions of men, after the rudiments of the world, and not after Christ. This should help you better understand that all thoughts, Words or information does not come from God."*

Facts vs. Truth

Facts and truth are not the same. Truth is an absolute and facts aren't. Facts relate to what is seen in the earth realm and truth abides in the realm that is unseen. When it comes to God, you cannot add to or take away from

> **Facts relate to what is seen in the earth realm and truth abides in the realm that is unseen.**

anything he's said. He is God and cannot lie; however men can. I believe that this is what has caused many to doubt the voice of God and reject the prophetic. When you reject the prophetic, you reject the mind of God. When you reject the mind of God, you will experience stagnation and frustration.

Jesus came to show us the thoughts of the Father, and the evidence of what he said and did brought forth the manifestation of what he spoke. When you operate with a higher mindset, it opens a place in the supernatural for you to receive the tools needed to manifest God's divine will for you and your family. Then, you will become a change agent and a person with the potential of being a global influencer. Embracing the truth and the power of the Word of God is the only thing that will bring a radical change in your thinking and thus your life.

God wants us to reign victoriously on the earth. While we can discern that the return of Jesus is very near, we have to shift our focus from going to heaven, because the Lord has empowered us to establish heaven on earth. The mission of Jesus Christ was to make sure he re-opened the spiritual portals to give us a way back to the mind of God.

> **The only reason we contend with problems in the earth is because we don't have a prophetic mindset.**

I submit to you the only reason we contend with problems in the earth is because we don't have a prophetic mindset. A prophetic mindset leads you to solutions, allows you to remain encouraged in the middle of storms, it gives you confidence in God's ability to do *"Exceeding abundantly above all that we ask or think, according to the power that worketh in us."* There is a power that works in us- a supernatural and prophetic power.

Short-Term and Long-Term Memory

The mind is interesting thing to study. If I were not called into ministry, I think I would have been a psychologist. I love to study the mind and to analyze people, to understand the "why" behind what people do. At any rate, in my research of the brain and the human mind, I found that there are two kinds of memory the brains stores: short-term and long-term.

Short-term memory is when an electro chemical occurrence takes place in the brain, that takes a picture but it doesn't become fixed or locked in. Long-term memory reinforces things by meditation and repetition causing it to be locked into your consciousness (your awareness). A process called protein synthesis occurs whereby the memory becomes biologically a part of your brain cells. This is how you can become one, or so interconnected (spiritually and psychologically) with the things of your past.

The effects of short and long term memory produce thoughts that are in your head (mind). However, the true essence of a person originates from the treasuries of the heart and not the head as stated in Psalm 23:7, *"For as he thinketh in his heart, so is he: Eat and drink, saith he to thee; but his heart is not with thee."*

It is so important for the mind of the heart and the mind of the head to connect and be in agreement. When this happens, it will minimize frustration in our lives, because what we speak forth- either through prophecy, confession or even the Word of God- we will see it manifest. This is how the human mind works: if we have experienced things that produce rejection, fear, hopelessness, bitterness, and un forgiveness, then the mind, because of the memory that is stores, will go to work to block those feelings. Even if a new scenario is presented, acceptance of new thoughts of faith and truth will be complicated.

THE POWER OF A PROPHETIC MINDSET

> *Casting down imaginations, and every high thing that exalteth itself against the knowledge of God, and bringing into captivity every thought to the obedience of Christ;*   -- **2 Corinthians 2:5 KJV**

Can you see why, prophetically, God wants you to come up higher to uproot, tear down and demolish everything that is contrary to His mind?

What you meditate on the most creates your long term memory. This is why we are admonished to constantly think on the word. Having a life filled with good success not only depends on what we think about, but it is directly connected to meditating on the Word of God.

> *This book of the law shall not departs out of thy mouth; but thou shalt meditate therein day and night, that thou mayest observe to do according to all that is written therein: for then thou shalt make thy way prosperous, and then thou shalt have good success.*   -- **Joshua 1:8 KJV**

Faith: The Gateway to Higher Thinking

Faith is the bridge that leads us over to a higher prophetic way of thinking. For just a moment, I want you to release a sound into the atmosphere by declaring aloud "Lord I need greater faith." Faith is demonstrating trust and believing God when there is no evidence that He can or will produce anything for you. Scary isn't it? Many of us love God, but, find it hard to trust him because our past experiences with people. People are what God uses to birth greatness in us. If you recall the story of Hannah, her rival Peninnah provoked her to a place in prayer to produce Israel's first prophet, who was also a priest, and the last judge. Hannah shows us the power of prayer and faith

> **Faith is the bridge that leads us over to a higher prophetic way of thinking.**

which caused her barren womb to produce life. We can't place God on the same level as man. God will never mistreat or abandon us.

> *For I know the thoughts and plans I have for you, says The Lord, thoughts and plans for welfare and peace and not for evil, to give you hope in your final outcome.*   **-- Jeremiah 29:11 Amplified**

God's thoughts about you will always be greater than the thoughts you have about yourself. The reason you think negative thoughts is directly connected to the negative sound that "fell out" of heaven when Satan got kicked out with a third of the angels. That negative sound that came from the dark realms was one full of pride and lies that manipulated the earth's atmosphere. When you sit and dwell in negative sounds, they will cultivate negative seed-thoughts making it difficult to receive truth.

Whenever a person's innocence is taken it's hard to get it back. Adam and Eve never knew that they were naked until they had been stripped of their innocence. Genesis 3:11 supports this, *"And he said, who told you that you were naked? Have you eaten from the tree that I commanded you not to eat from?"* When you open yourself up to what you believe, is truth only to find it was deception, the mind will have difficulty processing that truth once you actually hear it. Whether short or long term, your memory has committed the deception which makes the heart unwilling to receive.

All of us, at some point, have been victims of deception. Either we have either been deceived or we have deceived others. Until you become resolute about changing, you will be stagnant. You must let go of the things that have held you captive for too long. Ask the Lord to help you forgive and release people who have done bad things to you, because in the next season of your life you need to be free. Years ago, the Lord revealed to me that when you don't forgive, it's like living at the scene of the crime. God doesn't want you to live this way any longer. Trust him and come all the way into a life of purpose which leads you into a higher way of living. Starting today, you must be willing to leave where you are: I speak to you prophetically that you become free from the memory of every setback in your life. Setbacks are merely opportunities for comebacks for the child of God. With child-like faith, I want you to climb into the arms of Daddy God, trust Him to take you to new levels; to launch out into the deep, to climb new mountains and soar to new heights.

Mountain Climbing

Who may ascend the mountain of the Lord? Who may stand in his holy place? The one who clean hands and a pure heart, who does not trust in an idol or swear by a false god.

-- Psalm 24:3-4 NIV

The rhema word is "a thing spoken." It is God's thought that is spoken with power to those that are willing to separate their lives unto holiness and righteousness. The rhema word comes out of the realm of faith and everyone isn't willing to do what is required to access this network of truth. I like to think of it as God's media mountain. Climbing a mountain takes hard work. Before you can go mountain climbing you must have the proper gear. The proper gear would be the whole or full armor of God.

Wherefore take unto you the whole armour of God, that ye may be able to withstand in the evil day, and having done all, to stand. Stand therefore, having your loins girt about with truth, and having on the breastplate of righteousness; And your feet shod with the preparation of the gospel of peace; Above all, taking the shield of faith, wherewith ye shall be able to quench all the fiery darts of the wicked. And take the helmet of salvation, and the word of the Spirit, which is the Word of God: Praying always with all prayer and supplication in the Spirit, and watching thereunto with all perseverance and supplication for all saints;

-- Ephesians 6:13-18 KJV

A HIGHER WAY OF THINKING

The higher you go in your spirit-led life, the more opposition and enemies you will encounter along the journey. David, through his process to become king, could attest to this truth. Moreover, when you use the spiritual armour listed above, God will automatically send supernatural reinforcement to assist in the climb and to protect you from the hits and pitfalls.

Mountain climbing is strategic and the first thing you've got to know is not everyone can go with you up the mountain when it's time for you to ascend. I gave a prophetic word at the beginning of this year, and the Lord told me that in 2014, there would be such an outpouring for the righteous. Some of you have been so connected to people, places, and things that have weighed you down. In this shift, God is separating the wheat from the tare and he is only obligated to bless those who are covenantly connected to him. Don't be surprised or look for certain people who cannot partake of the blessings of God in your ascension.

> **Make a decision to disconnect from the familiar and walk in faith.**

As the Lord told Samuel, "How long will you mourn for Saul, since I have rejected him as king over Israel? Fill your horn with oil and be on your way; I am sending you to Jesse of Bethlehem. I have chosen one of his sons to be king." (I Samuel 16:1) Many of the people we try to take with us on our journey are neither called nor qualified to go to the next level with us. While it hurts and may be a little frightening, God has moved on from people who refuse to change and obey him. As a rule, we are creatures of habit and comfort. God is doing "suddenlies," which means things around our lives are changing quickly to reposition players. The repositioning is really an alignment to get everyone in their proper positions for the blessing. With this being said, there is no need to allow fear to creep in. I promise you,

THE POWER OF A PROPHETIC MINDSET

that when you make a decision to disconnect from the familiar and walk in faith, there will be an audience waiting to join you.

I have learned and I hope this helps you, that sometimes the scars of the past and the memories they hold, make you believe that you are not a mountain climber. They speak to us through the subconscious places of the mind to tell us to just keep our feet on the ground and to never try to go higher. As you use the keys to cultivate a prophetic mindset, the Spirit of Christ will give you the supernatural favor to cause doors to open and increase flow towards you. At this point, you will be able to mount up with wings like an eagle and soar. If you want to live a high- life full of power and unlimited possibilities you must remember that what God requires of you may not make sense. Faith doesn't have to make sense because obedience releases the blessing.

Just like we can't see the air, nor do we understand where it comes from, we know that it exists. Jesus did an illogical thing by spitting into clay-in essence making a mud pie - to give sight to a blind man. All of the miracles Jesus performed came from a supernatural realm of power that made no sense. I believe what God desires to demonstrate, is that once we connect our faith to prophecy everything in the earth will be made available for us to display His handiwork. If you are living in this 21st century, and have made it to see this dispensational shift into the kingdom, then you have the awesome privilege of knowing God's mind so that mountains-the high places- that produce higher prophetic thinking will be where you live every day.

CHAPTER 6

THE PROPHETIC SPIRIT

Now the Word of the LORD came to me saying, Before I formed you in the womb I knew you, And before you were born I consecrated you; I have appointed you a prophet to the nations."
Jeremiah 1:4-5 ESV

KEY TERMS

Portal [15] - An egress for traversing back and forth and for transporting products sent between two locations. Spiritually, that would be between two worlds

Supernatural [16] - That which operates and controls our natural world from the spiritual world above our own.

Everything we see in the earth represents a thought that God had. Think about this, if you own a car, the car represents God's thought concerning you being able to be transported from one place to another. Before you purchase a car from a dealership, it will have every component to make the car function according to the design of the manufacturer. Things like an engine, a steering wheel, tires, brakes, etc. Without these

THE POWER OF A PROPHETIC MINDSET

things and others a car will not function according the original purpose. Likewise, before time as we know it began, God created and equipped us with everything we need to operate as powerful prophetic agents. In Jeremiah 1:4-5, the prophetic word was released declaring Jeremiah would be appointed to be a prophet before he was born.

> *God created and equipped us with everything we need to operate as powerful prophetic agents.*

Further, the word explains that before he was even placed in his mother's womb, God predetermined that he would have a spirit that contained prophetic tools, operations, and functions, allowing him to fulfill the purpose of being ordained as a prophet.

> *Prophetic realms are the areas of concentration or mastery where God gives you dominion and rulership.*

The spirit of every living creature comes from God. You can change the outward appearance of something, but it won't change the spirit of it. The spirit of a man is the spirit of a man. Even if you dress him like a woman, the spirit of the man is still present. When God created the fish, within its anatomy he designed it to have gills, fins and scales to be able to swim under water. I am laying this foundation so that you will be able to understand the uniqueness of the prophetic spirit and how it is specific to those who are called to operate in prophetic realms. Prophetic realms are the areas of concentration or mastery where God gives you dominion and rulership to operate in authority to utilize your spiritual and supernatural tools (your prophetic resources.)

Comprehending the Prophetic Spirit

As you grow prophetically, you will begin to notice a new awareness of spiritual and supernatural things developing in your life. Just like any process in life, there are stages of development which prepare you to fully understand and exercise the power contained within the prophetic spirit.

Awareness

The awareness or awakening stage is where you begin to see your life take on a new perspective. When babies discover their voice, fingers and toes, they begin to become fixated by those new discoveries. Upon the discovery, they immediately begin to exercise the operations of each of those functions. In like manner, in the prophetic, everything becomes magnified as you begin to have a greater sensitivity to what is being developed in your prophetic spirit. You could say that the awakening of your prophetic spirit causes things to become super-sized because; you begin to see what can't be seen with the natural eyes, and hear what can't be heard with the natural ears. The awakening of your prophetic spirit gives you upgrades which enables you to travel in supernatural dimensions and access power that others don't have. It is like having a line of communication extended to you from another world that is not seen with the physical eyes but is seen with the eyes of the spirit.

> *The awareness or awakening stage is where you begin to see your life take on a new perspective.*

Prophetic people are born with supernatural capabilities which qualify them to carry out their life assignments professionally and informally through their gifts, talents and abilities. These prophetic abilities include day and night visions, dreams, dream interpretation, hearing supernatural communications when ministering to people regarding their history, hurts and hopes, receiving and delivering prophecy, decrees and declarations, prayer, intercession, and praise and worship to name a few. When you begin to understand the depth of God's prophetic treasuries, how you function in every area of your life will change. Additionally, your mindset will be expanded from focusing on prophecy and prophesying as the benchmarks of the prophetic to grasp the full spectrum of the spiritual spheres.

This is a side note but I feel that it's important to share a revelation the Lord gave me concerning the connection between the eyes and the ears. Prophets and prophetic types receive communications like: dreams, visions, prophecies, by what they see in the spirit or what they hear by the spirit. This is why when God speaks you will get pictures or images to correspond with what He has said. When I teach and minister, I often say "It's not that you see God... that you see God, but it's that you hear God... that you see God. You see what I'm saying?" Therefore, if you are going to see seemingly impossible situations change, you have to draw a line and use the Word of God as a prophecy to speak, decree, and declare until the prophecy comes to pass.

Prophetic Gifts

Brothers and sisters, I want you to know about the gifts of the Holy Spirit. You know that at one time you were unbelievers. You were somehow drawn away to worship statues of gods that couldn't even speak. So I tell you that no one who is speaking with the help of God's Spirit says, "May Jesus be cursed." And without the help of the Holy Spirit no one can say, "Jesus is Lord." There are different kinds of gifts. But they are all given by the same Spirit. There are different ways to serve. But they all come from the same Lord. There are different ways to work. But the same God makes it possible for all of us to have all those different things. The Holy

THE PROPHETIC SPIRIT

Spirit is given to each of us in a special way. That is for the good of all. To some people the Spirit gives the message of wisdom. To others the same Spirit gives the message of knowledge. To others the same Spirit gives faith. To others that one Spirit gives gifts of healing. To others he gives the power to do miracles. To others he gives the ability to prophesy. To others he gives the ability to tell the spirits apart. To others he gives the ability to speak in different kinds of languages they had not known before. And to still others he gives the ability to explain what was said in those languages. All of the gifts are produced by one and the same Spirit. He gives them to each person, just as he decides. -- **Romans 12:1-11 NIRV**

Prophetic gifts are confined to the Holy Spirit's manifestations. While the prophet can prophesy at will, the prophetic gift is mostly restricted to prophesying by the unction of the Holy Spirit. Once the word, be it a word of

> **Prophetic gifts are confined to the Holy Spirit's manifestations.**

knowledge or a word of wisdom is given, the extent of the prophetic gifts job has ended because they don't have the causative power which is weight, rank or clout in the spirit to activate the word.

Contrary to popular belief, you can't go to a university or seminary- or even have someone lay hands on you- to become a prophet. Neither can a human vessel in the form of five-fold officers (Apostles, Prophets, Evangelists, Pastors, and Teachers), intercessors or prayer warriors give you a prophetic anointing. Prophetic gifts can do a lot of what the prophet does however they lack the enforcement license. For example, a security officer can make sure that people abide by the law but they generally don't have the power to arrest someone if a law is broken. Military officers have rank and a different type of latitude and freedom than a non- ranking solider. The higher the rank, the more accessibility the officer has to classified information and other high ranking governmental officials like the President.

All prophetic gifts are not officers, but all officers have prophetic gifts. The presence of spiritual gifts doesn't certify you as a prophet. Prophetic giftings are given to people from all walks of life that work and serve in many different capacities. They include fashion designers, dancers, engineers, ministers, athletes, and entertainers. Prophetic gifts are not locked inside of the church. Have you ever wondered why God did that? I believe that it is because He wanted his supernatural power to invade every realm, sphere, territory and domain in the earth. Overall, prophetic gifts are given to help support, encourage, edify, and comfort the body of Christ. The earth is in travail waiting for the sons (mature believers) who are in perfect sync with God, to see like Jesus saw, hear like Jesus heard and act like Jesus did. (John 5:19)

> ***All prophetic gifts are not officers, but all officers have prophetic gifts.***

The Prophet's Spirit

You are born with a prophet's spirit and this is what makes a prophet a prophet. A prophet is a person who has been given a license to go in and out of the spiritual spheres and speak forth that which is seen and heard in terrains of heaven. As a mouthpiece, the prophet is assigned a supernatural delegation of angels to execute and implement the will, heart, intentions and purposes of the Lord. The prophet's spirit gives you the ability to connect to God's mind and adapt to his form of communication. The amount of time prophets spend with God in their development process helps to mold them into oneness with God. The prophet is an integral part of God's kingdom staff. Their job duties include equipping and training the Body of Christ to come into the full measure of Christ as well as governing, guarding and guiding Christ's New Testament church.

Psychics

For the gifts and calling of God are without repentance
-- Romans 11:29 KJV

The gifts and callings of God are without repentance which means that the gifts or supernatural abilities that God gives are irrevocable. If God endows you with a gift, He doesn't take back the gift, even if you don't submit it to him for use. A few years ago, I engaged my students in an interesting conversation on the occult realm which deals with psychics, clairvoyants, spiritists, necromancers, and soothsayers. We were discussing prophets and false prophets and I asked them whether they thought that psychics were prophets. Their responses were varied but my conclusion was that most of them didn't think that psychics were prophets.

As a point of clarity, psychics are prophets. They, like prophets of the Lord, are born with a prophetic spirit but they have chosen to use their gift for Satan. Psychics forecast Satan's mind. They tell the future by occultic means by reading your soul through the carnal spheres. Anytime a person promotes the flesh, or carnal activity, they are incapable of giving you God's mind concerning you; they can only give you Satan's mind which comes out of the second heaven- information that is already in the earth. On the other hand, prophets are wired to access Gods thoughts and intents quicker than others do. They don't have to rely on what is familiar like psychics because they are in line with God's communication systems because of how God constructs them.

Prophesy

The hand of the LORD was upon me, and carried me out in the spirit of the LORD, and set me down in the midst of the valley which was full of bones, And caused me to pass by them round about: and, behold, there

THE POWER OF A PROPHETIC MINDSET

were very many in the open valley; and, lo, they were very dry. And he said unto me, Son of man, can these bones live? And I answered, O Lord GOD, thou knowest. Again he said unto me, Prophesy upon these bones, and say unto them, O ye dry bones, hear the Word of the LORD. Thus saith the Lord GOD unto these bones; Behold, I will cause breath to enter into you, and ye shall live: And I will lay sinews upon you, and will bring up flesh upon you, and cover you with skin, and put breath in you, and ye shall live; and ye shall know that I am the LORD. So I prophesied as I was commanded: and as I prophesied, there was a noise, and behold a shaking, and the bones came together, bone to his bone. And when I beheld, lo, the sinews and the flesh came up upon them, and the skin covered them above: but there was no breath in them. Then said he unto me, Prophesy unto the wind, prophesy, son of man, and say to the wind, Thus saith the Lord GOD; Come from the four winds, O breath, and breathe upon these slain, that they may live. So I prophesied as he commanded me, and the breath came into them, and they lived, and stood up upon their feet, an exceeding great army. Then he said unto me, Son of man, these bones are the whole house of Israel: behold, they say, Our bones are dried, and our hope is lost: we are cut off for our parts. Therefore prophesy and say unto them, Thus saith the Lord GOD; Behold, O my people, I will open your graves, and cause you to come up out of your graves, and bring you into the land of Israel. And ye shall know that I am the LORD, when I have opened your graves, O my people, and brought you up out of your graves, And shall put my spirit in you, and ye shall live, and I shall place you in your own land: then shall ye know that I the LORD have spoken it, and performed it, saith the LORD.

-- Ezekiel 37:1-14 KJV

I would be remiss not to talk about the gift that in my opinion has branded the prophetic. Prophesying sets things in motion in the spirit realm because God desires for something to be accomplished here on earth. There is a voice within the voice of prophecy that speaks to all of creation to cause it to hear and respond when God speaks. Ezekiel prophesied to the dry bones, as he was instructed by the Lord and something supernatural took place. The dry bones recognized the sound of their Creator through Ezekiel's voice and began to come alive and come together to become a great army instead of dead mass of people with no home. When you prophesy, what seems to be impossible becomes possible, what appears hopeless is infused with hope, what is dead comes back to life, what is broken is mended and restored and that which is sick is healed! Glory to God, no matter what it looks like, God's word (the prophetic word) is quick, and powerful, and sharper than any two-edged sword, piercing even to the dividing asunder of soul and spirit, and of the joints and marrow, and is a discerner of the thoughts and intents of the heart. (Hebrews 4:12)

> **There is a voice within the voice of prophecy that speaks to all of creation to cause it to hear and respond when God speaks.**

CHAPTER 7

THE MIND OF PROPHECY

Follow after charity, and desire spiritual gifts, but rather that ye may prophesy.
I Corinthians 14:1 KJV

KEY TERMS

Revelatory [17] - That which emanates from, or emerges as, a revelation of God's truth as found in His Word.

Revelation [18] - The disclosed Word of God

Prophecy is one of the most potent resources of the prophetic and it comes from the predictive spheres. The predictive spheres give you the ability to enter into the spirit realm and get foreknowledge on your circumstance and say to it what God says so you can win. Prophecy as "an inspired communication from God. Prophecy is

> *Prophecy is one of the most potent resources of the prophetic and it comes from the predictive spheres.*

God's supernatural communications media. What makes it prophecy is that God speaks through men and women before earthly events in question occur." (Paula A. Price, The Prophet's Dictionary) This is why it is predictive because it deals with what is going to happen ahead of time. It is important to establish this because when I speak of prophecy I'm not using a synonym for the word prophetic. I have found that most people confuse the words "prophetic" and "prophecy" because, while they sound very similar, they have different meanings. The prophetic is the portal that opens the door to prophecy.

> *Prophecy and prophesying go hand in hand, one involves hearing and the other involves saying.*

In 1 Corinthians 14:1, the Apostle Paul admonishes us to: *"Follow after charity, and desire spiritual gifts, but rather that ye may prophesy."* The message Paul gave to the Corinthian church was simple; first pursue love, and then desire spiritual gifts. Above all of the gifts however, let your desire for prophecy outweigh them all. I believe that Paul said this because prophecy is a direct connection to hear what God is saying. Once you receive God's communication through prophecy you can then prophesy it over earth's affairs. Prophecy and prophesying go hand in hand, one involves hearing and the other involves saying. When you prophesy you are speaking forth the revealed mind of God on a matter.

The Purpose and Function of Prophecy

God has a divine plan for everyone and in order for those plans to be accomplished there has to be a medium or a method in which He gets the job done. The primary purpose for prophecy is to uncover and unveil, to make (previously unknown information) known to others. The spiritual instrument of prophecy is what God uses to speak from the revelatory realms of heaven to and through His prophets and prophetic types. The revelatory realm is where spiritual knowledge is stored until there is a demand or need for it to be released in the earth. In this realm, things already exist; however, the igniting of prophecy causes there to be a transfer or exchange of the mind of God in the earth. So, a prophecy's function is to transfer the thoughts of God through the voice of man; to interject God's will through a series of events that He orchestrates for the good of man. When a prophetic word goes forth, things must automatically shift and change and conform to what God has spoken from the revelatory realms.

> **Prophecy's function is to transfer the thoughts of God through the voice of man; to interject God's will through a series of events that He orchestrates for the good of man.**

> *Death and life are in the power of the tongue: and they that love it shall eat the fruit thereof.*   **-- Proverbs 18:21 KJV**

This scripture is saying that your tongue frames your world. God gives everyone the ability to create, build or tear down. You can either choose to speak life which is prophesying a prophecy from God or you can speak death which is prophesying a prophecy from Satan. When you fully understand what I just said, you will be diligent about what you release from your mouth, and guarding your eyes and ears. The things that you see and hear produce the images which affect what you believe.

We are admonished to guard our and eyes and ears. There is an old saying which goes, "Seeing is believing." When you believe what you see, it will be what you say . . . this is called prophetic assassination. Prophetic

THE POWER OF A PROPHETIC MINDSET

assassination is uttering negative words that can be used against someone to judge, condemn to failure, or defeat. Proverbs 6:2 says, *"you have been trapped by what you said, ensnared by the words of your mouth."*

As a prophetic person, you must be careful about what you say because words spoken in jest have the potential to come to pass. Remember, your world is being framed every day. It is highly possible that you are solely responsible for your position in life. You could have said, or are saying, things right now that could be weaving a web around your hands and feet to slow down or stop your progress. The main point, that I want you to get is if you never meet a prophet or receive a prophetic word from someone with a prophetic gift; it is your words of prophecy - those you speak to and about yourself - which can either cause you the greatest harm, or open the biggest door for you to enter into your promise. God gave you the power to choose your destiny.

> *In the beginning God created the heavens and the earth. Now the earth was formless and empty, darkness was over the surface of the deep, and the spirit of God was hovering over the waters. And God said, "let there be light," and there was light. Here we see that before the world was God said, "let there be...." And it was.* — **Genesis 1:1-3**

When the world was formed, it contained no light. Even though God's original intent was for there to be light in the earth, darkness still covered the earth. God himself spoke light into existence and it manifested. The incredible thing about prophecy is that when it is spoken, it must come to pass. The prophet Samuel is a perfect example of this as the Words says in I Samuel 3:19 "And Samuel grew, and the LORD was with him, and did let none of his words fall to the ground." There is potency and power in the prophetic word. God cares so much prophecy that he emphatically declares about his word , *"So is my word that goes out from my mouth: It will not return to me empty, but will accomplish what I desire and achieve the purpose for which I sent it."* (Isaiah 55:11)

THE MIND OF PROPHECY

Now that we have gotten a clearer understanding of prophecy, let's go back and revisit what the Apostle Paul said in I Corinthians 14:1 "...but rather that you may prophesy". I believe that he is saying that when you desire to prophesy, you are joining the ranks of those who cause things to manifest and come into total alignment with Heaven's agenda. The prophetic word carries within it a birth certificate and death certificate. So when you prophesy, the prophecy will cause some things to be birthed and others to die. Remember, nothing just appears or shows up in the earth until God uses someone to prophesy it in the earth.

Prophetic Accuracy

The term prophetic accuracy defines the prophet's skill in accurately delivering the Word of the Lord. It includes the obligation to not veer from the word of the Lord in order to assure the cooperation and compliance of his or her angelic delegation. This is what distinguishes a true prophet from a false prophet.[19] This is crucial when delivering a word to the people on the behalf of God. He is a keeper of His word but He is not obligated to fulfill our words.

The Lord told Samuel specifically, that He wouldn't allow any of his words to fall to the ground. He did this because, He knew Samuel was a man of order and operated within his boundaries and prophetic authority. I have found, especially with P.I.T.'s (Prophets in Training) and those who are growing prophetically, the need to try to impress or please people. This is when they start adlibbing, like singers do, when they want to extend a song. I overemphasized to my students that exactness and accuracy are vitally important in the prophetic. It is never about how much is said, rather if what is said, comes from the Lord.

This is a classic example of the danger of "winging a prophecy." A few years ago, one of my students asked me a question concerning a prophecy they had received from a prophet. The prophecy included a time frame for something to happen and it never did. If God doesn't establish a timeframe for a prophetic word and a prophetic vessel does, it can create spiritual interference, or a hindrance, in the process of that word being fulfilled. I want to caution you: if God isn't specific-he doesn't need help. It may simply mean that a person has to participate in the process of the word being fulfilled. By this, I mean there may be specific instructions to follow and strict obedience will determine the outcome of the word.

Faith and Prophecy

Prophecy is a gift of the spirit; and in order for the utterance to occur, faith must be present. I like to think of faith as the fuel that causes the prophecy to be released. Faith is essential in the prophetic realms because faith is the catalyst that causes things to move.

> *Having then gifts differing according to the grace that is given to us, whether prophecy, let us prophesy according to the proportion of faith.*
> **-- Romans 12:6 KJV**

The bible says that we prophesy according to the measure of faith. The Lord revealed to me that faith builds a cloud in the heavens which prepares prophecy to be released. Just like a cloud is formed before rain is released, the bigger the cloud the more rain it holds. God causes your faith to build what I call prophetic clouds where He stores up what you need. The size of your cloud depends on the size of your faith. Once you begin to operate in the realm of faith you can access the mind of God and then open up your mouth to prophesy what you see and hear prophetically to cause it to move from heaven to materialize in the earth. Once you begin to operate in the realm of faith you can access the mind of God and then open up your mouth to prophesy what you see and hear prophetically to cause it to move from heaven to materialize in the earth. Remember, faith doesn't make sense, it's supernatural.

Opponents of Prophecy

When faith is present you can move mountains. On the other hand, where doubt exists in your life, the enemy creates a playground to frustrate and taunt you. Doubt opens the door for you to cultivate a different mindset, one that is filled with uncertainty, disbelief, insecurity, unbelief and the like. This leads us to becoming double-minded and double mindedness causes instability.

We are instructed to find out what pleases God. Without faith it is impossible to please God. Simply put, you can't please God when doubt is present or if you have a mindset which suggests that you have to see something before you believe it. This is what doubting Thomas did when he couldn't comprehend Jesus being raised from the dead. Thomas was a part of Jesus' ministry. He was there to witness the supernatural and the miraculous yet doubt prevented him from receiving what was going on around him. Maybe many of us, like Thomas, hang around the things of God watching carefully to draw a conclusion about the power and the glory of the Kingdom of God. The greatest enemies against you embracing a prophetic mindset are the spirits of doubt and fear. Doubt and fear will always stand to block your faith and prevent you from entering into the prophetic which is the realm of faith and miracles.

From church leaders and corporate executives, to those who hold management and supervisory positions I have noticed that the spirit of fear governs decisions that are made. I am not against order, in fact, my apostolic mantle is strongly administrative; however, whenever you find strict and stringent guidelines in business or ministry under the guise of order, it is usually derived from a spirit of fear - manifesting as control.

Here's the deal, fear tells you not to trust and doubt tells you not to believe. Fear's mission is to make you believe you are in control instead of trusting and knowing God is control. Even our salvation is based on trust and belief. Trusting God is the demonstration of your love for him that causes you to obey. Doubt, on the other hand, is like a little leaven that spoils the whole loaf. When you doubt God, what you are saying to him is that: "I am not convinced that you are who you say you are and that you can do what you said you can do." The prophetic word meets you at your place of faith, so begin to exercise your faith muscles and remove all doubt to walk into a new dimension of possibilities in God. I say to you prophetically that as you begin to faith God, new doors will begin to open for you and things that have been previously locked down will be released. Even when you are unsure and the enemy presents fear as a choice "speak to those things that be not as though they were" and watch the increase, overflow and favor God releases into your life.

CHAPTER 8

PROPHETIC PRAYER

Jesus answered and said unto them, Verily I say unto you, If ye have faith, and doubt not, ye shall not only do this [which is done] to the fig tree, but also if ye shall say unto this mountain, Be thou removed, and be thou cast into the sea; it shall be done. And all things, whatsoever ye shall ask in prayer, believing, ye shall receive..

Matthew 21:21-22 KJV

KEY TERMS

Authority [20] - the power to give orders or make decisions: the power or right to direct or control someone or something.

Sphere [21] - an arena or region of influence or activity that is more figurative than literal. A Word for the immaterial territories of influence and control embedded in creation.

Heaven is constantly invading the earth and the most common means is through prophetic prayer. Prophetic prayer is conducted by the prophet or prophetic types with the express purpose of compelling the manifestation of a prophecy. It always has intercessory overtones and

THE POWER OF A PROPHETIC MINDSET

exhibits strong authoritative commands to spiritual forces others usually cannot see. They require relentless faith and are strategic and tactical in nature.[22]

When we pray prophetically we are praying the kingdom's agenda. We are praying from heaven perspective and not earth's perspective, declaring out of the predictive spheres what will happen at the appointed time. Prayer in and of itself can be considered God's supernatural and spiritual network, which allows us to tune into the mind of God. Prophetic prayer lets us travel outside of time into the spirit realm to get our personal promises and bring them back to the earth. Therefore, when we are praying prophetically, we are praying solutions and not problems; because in the spirit realm, God shows us every need met, every hurt healed, and freedom for every place of bondage.

> **When we pray prophetically we are praying the kingdom's agenda.**

The Lord said to me that nothing moves from heaven until there is a request made from the earth. In Matthew 6: 9-13 *(we will discuss in greater detail)*, the disciples asked Jesus to teach them how to pray. The Lord's Prayer, which is a prophetic prayer, was Jesus giving the disciples the kingdom order for legal exchange to take place in the earth. The first order of prayer is for the kingdom to come, which means you are calling and directing God's government, rule and authority into earth affairs. It also means " not my will your will be done". When you pray this, it lets the Father know you have completely surrendered to His way of thinking and resolving all matters. When you cry out to God for help, the position of your heart must be "I'm moving out of the way and letting you handle this." If you ask someone to help you, it only makes sense for you to step aside and allow them to help.

PROPHETIC PRAYER

I think it's crazy at times that we call on the Father to help us and then we don't remove our hands out of the situation. As a Chief Apostolic prophet, I counsel a lot of people. Over the years, many have come to me for counsel and after I provided godly wisdom they never applied it to their situations. The funny thing is that although they have been given a prescription for their problem and didn't apply it, they still wonder why things haven't changed. I can only image the Father's position when we ask him to intervene on our behalf and after he shows up we say to ourselves "I didn't think God would really do it." This is why Jesus instructs us to pray the prayer of faith. Because, I believe, it shows God we are serious about him bringing the solution and that we will step back allow him move on our behalf.

Prayer and Faith

> **A heart that is filled with faith will change the trajectory of your prophetic prayers.**

A heart that is filled with faith will change the trajectory of your prophetic prayers. First of all it demonstrates that you are convinced, that God can and will do what he said.

Faith gives you access into the prophetic spheres and whenever you pray prophetic prayers, you are bringing God thoughts into your now. Hebrews 11:1 affirms, "Now faith is the substance of things hoped for, the evidence of things not seen." Faith is always now, meaning in your present situation, if it's not now then it's not faith.

Too often people say I am "believing" God but what they fail to understand is that as long as they are "believing" it prolongs their promise from coming. Recently, as I was traveling home from a ministry engagement the Lord spoke to me concerning the difference between "believing" and "believe." He told me that when you say you are believing me for something that doesn't represent faith because you haven't settled in your heart that it is already done because believing suggests you are building up the courage to trust.

The word "believe" on the other hand is a declarative word and it suggests that you are convinced and have settled on what you are standing for. Belief says "I trust you" you Lord and that's the bottom line. Jesus said when I return will I find faith in the earth?

Each one of us has been given a measure of faith, meaning God gave everyone just enough of His mind to give us hope. Hope causes you not to give up. The Lord told me "hope keeps you focused when you can't see anything with your natural eyes. It keeps you in a posture of expectation, searching daily, for what you heard God said he would give you." From this point on, when God says you are healed don't look for the sickness. Hope should spring up everyday to remind you to believe and to look for your healing instead of sickness.

A Birthing Chamber

Whenever God gets ready to bring something new into our lives he ignites the desire to pray in us, because he wants to communicate and commune with us. In prayer God downloads strategies and blue prints for what he wants to accomplish. It is also the place where you get to see the true issues of the heart. The reason you need to deal with your heart issues is because they can hinder your prayers.

> *In prayer God downloads strategies and blue prints for what he wants to accomplish.*

Prophetic Prayer

Prophetic prayer is causative and reactionary so I want to leave you with a road map to be successful in your prophetic journey. There are four components of prophetic prayer. I like to refer to them as ingredients because each is essential for powerful prophetic prayer. The first component or ingredient is praise and worship associated with it. The second is petition which is a request made for something desired, especially a respectful or humble request, as to a superior or to one of those in authority; a supplication or prayer. The third is penitence which is a feeling of regret for one's sins; or feeling repentance. The fourth and final component of prophetic prayer is proclamation which is declaring.

> *After this manner therefore pray ye: Our Father which art in heaven, Hallowed be thy name. Thy kingdom come, Thy will be done in earth, as it is in heaven. Give us this day our daily bread. And forgive us our debts, as we forgive our debtors. And lead us not into temptation, but deliver us from evil: For thine is the kingdom, and the power, and the glory, forever. Amen* **-- Matthew 6:9-13 KJV**

Praise, petition, penitence and prophetic proclamation are all in the Lord's prayer. Let's start with praise and worship. Jesus said you must pray this way, "Our Father in heaven, hallowed (to hallow something is to show honor and reverence.)" This is praise and worship. You start with praise. In Psalm 22:3 David said, "But You are holy, O You that inhabits the praises of Israel." David knew all about praise. God inhabits the praises of His people.

Ingredient #1

Praise and Worship

About five years ago, the Lord spoke to me and told me that he was building Glory Domes. This revelation was amazing because he said that he was longer building churches. These Glory Domes would be built with prayer, praise and worship. The foundation is prayer, the walls are praise and the roof is worship.

The power in praise and worship goes beyond what you could imagine. You can never experience authentic worship without praise because produces worship. Praise means to speak well of God and to acknowledge what He has done; true praise-beyond the flesh- invokes God's presence. When you want God to intervene, create an atmosphere of praise. Psalm 22:3 says: *"God inhabits the praises of His people,"* so when God's people praise Him, He draws near and worship results.

God's presence comes through our praise. If we desire to live an abundant lifestyle, we must learn to cultivate a continual environment of praise.

> *I will I will bless the LORD at all times: his praise shall continually be in my mouth.*   **-- Psalm 34:1 KJV**

As you bless the Lord, his praise will consume you to the point where you won't have time to focus on anything but his goodness. Hebrews 13:15 says, *"Through Jesus, therefore, let us continually offer to God a sacrifice of praise- the fruit of lips that confess His name."*

Praise and worship will always attract the presence of God. The presence of God and getting the mind of God are so important to prophetic people. It's one thing to know of God's omnipresence (being present everywhere), but quite another to experience the reality of His personal presence every day. Before anything else, we need the presence and the glory of God. Everything else in life hinges upon God's prophecy, miracles, or otherwise. True praise is an exercise; a discipline that flows from a pure heart and a humble spirit. God wants us to be humble and not arrogant because of the power the prophetic wields. Praise takes the power away from you and creates a habitation in which God is pleased to dwell.

Further praise and worship brings success and victories in our lives.

> *So the people shouted when the priests blew with the trumpets: and it came to pass, when the people heard the sound of the trumpet, and the people shouted with a great shout, that the wall fell down flat, so that the people went up into the city, every man straight before him, and they took the city.* **-- Joshua 6:20 KJV**

Although in the passage of scripture in Joshua, it does not specifically state that the Israelites were praising God, the Hebrew Word "rua", which is here translated "shout" and "shouted", is the same Word used in Psalm 100:1 and Psalm 95:1 and translated "shout joyfully," or make a joyful noise." When you praise, God's presence and power will come down like it did with the walls of Jericho to flatten walls in your life. When praises go up, then the presence automatically comes down. This is why we say that when the praises go up, blessings come down.

Ingredient #2

Petition

A petition is a solemn supplication or request to a superior authority; an entreaty. It is Making or presenting a formal request to (an authority) with respect to a particular cause. If you are going to do anything by prayer, you're going to have to start by coming into the throne room. We understood that praise and worship is how we get God's attention because he seeks those...draws nigh to those who reverence him and worship him in Spirit and in Truth.

Praise and worship give you prophetic insight and sight. The higher you go; you begin to look down on your circumstances and what has limited you and kept you from soaring. When God reveals his mind on of your situation you can have peace and leave all fear, doubt and worry behind. Prophets and prophetic types have a very special ability to come into the presence of God because their spirits are in tune with God and they can see and hear in the Spirit. Remember the Word says, we must pray in faith.

> *Therefore I say to you, Whatever things you desire, when you pray believe that you receive them and you shall have them.* -- **Mark 11:24 KJV**

> *But without faith it is impossible to please him: for he that cometh to God must believe that he is, and that he is a rewarder of them that diligently seek him.* -- **Hebrews 11:1 KJV**

Prayer has to be made in faith. Although I spoke to you earlier about faith, here is another example. God is charging us to believe him because, if you do not believe that you are not going to receive what you pray for.

But actually this verse goes one step further. It doesn't say, "Believe that when you pray you're going to receive what you've prayed for." It says, "Whatever things you desire when you pray believe that you receive them." When did you receive them?" When you prayed. Faith is always past tense. Faith does not say, "Well, I am believing that God can provide my needs." Faith does not say, "I am believing that God wants to provide my needs." Faith does not say, "I am believing God is going to provide my needs." Faith is the currency of Heaven, which allows you to say: I believe God has provided my needs; It is done; It is mine; My needs are met; My family is restored, My loved ones are saved; I have a new job; or whatever it is you may want to petition God for. I have been granted my petitions.

Ingredient #3

(Re) Pentance or Penitence

The third ingredient of prophetic prayer is repentance or penitence. Penitence means confession of sin. Jesus said in the Lord's Prayer that we must pray, *"Forgive us our trespasses as we forgive those who trespass against us."* The prayer of repentance clears the heart.

> *Beloved if our heart does not condemn us then we have confidence towards God. And whatever we ask we receive from Him because we keep His commandments and do those things that are pleasing in His sight.*
> -- 1 John 3:21

If your heart does not condemn you, you will have confidence in God. This means that the opposite is true. When your heart condemns you, it will be hard to have confidence in God. Sin will always cause you to feel guilty before God so that you won't come boldly into His presence and ask anything. Sin is designed to strip your confidence towards God. A person cannot have confidence while under condemnation so the prayer of repentance clears the heart. *"There is therefore now no condemnation to those who are in Christ Jesus." Romans 8:1*

The prayer of repentance is really a prayer of confession of sin and brokenness before God. Psalm 66:18 says, if I regard iniquity in my heart, the Lord will not hear me. If I regard iniquity in my heart – literally means, "If you have seen iniquity in your heart." Prophetic people must be holy because without holiness we can't see God.

Ingredient #4

Prophetic Declaration/Proclamation

The final type of prayer is prophetic decrees and declarations. Jesus said, *"Pray this way. Our Father in Heaven, hallowed be Thy Name. Thy kingdom come, Thy will be done on earth as it is in heaven."* When the Lord said we are to say, *"Thy Kingdom come,"* He was saying we are to give forth a command, "Come Thy Kingdom! Come! Be done Thy will on the earth." We are called to pack power. When we get into the throne room we can issue decrees, just like kings. The authority and access God has given us allows us to pray down from the throne. Glory to God!

And hath raised us up together, and made us sit together in heavenly places in Christ Jesus: -- **Ephesians 2:6**

We are seated with Christ Jesus in heavenly places. We came back from death with him, and are seated with him in the heavens. When you pray prophetically, you stand in that place as God's spokesperson with full authority to speak forth his word into the earth.

PROPHETIC PRAYER

And I will give unto thee the keys of the kingdom of heaven: and whatsoever thou shalt bind on earth shall be bound in heaven: and whatsoever thou shalt loose on earth shall be loosed in heaven.
-- Matthew 16:19

So shall My Word be that goes forth out of My mouth; it shall not return to Me empty, but it shall accomplish that which I please, and it shall prosper in the thing for which I sent it. **-- Isaiah 55:11**

God's Word is going to go out and it's going to do its job. When prophetic proclamations are launched from God's mouth, they become spiritual missiles that are going to hit the target! When you utilize all of these ingredients in prophetic prayer, you must abandon all forms of fear and begin to boldly open your mouth to proclaim and declare the Word of God. No matter what you face, God intends for you to win and have good success. A prophetic mindset doesn't mean that you will not experience a few bumps in the road, but you now have the tools to equip you and the keys to gain access to the supernatural realms of power. What are you waiting for? Release your prophetic sound into the atmosphere and embrace the power of your new prophetic mindset.

PROPHETIC DECLARATION

I decree and declare that I can do all things through Christ who strengthens me. I am a part of a prophetic generation called to rule and reign with Christ Jesus in heavenly places. Because I am prophetic, I must guard the anointing on my life. I cannot go everywhere and do everything. No weapon formed against me shall prosper.

I am the head and not the tail; above only and not beneath. I am the healed of the Lord and the blessed of the Lord. I am a royal priesthood, holy, set aside and set apart for God's use. God has not given me the spirit of fear but power, love and a sound mind. Therefore, I am empowered to go and come boldly decreeing and declaring what should and shouldn't be in the earth.

I know who I am, I was created in the image of Christ, a prophetic seed is in my belly, whatever I bind on the earth...shall be bound in heaven. Whatever I loose on the earth...it shall be loosed. I have the supernatural power of God working in me. I will do miracles and signs and wonders shall follow me. Because I know the Lord, I will do great exploits. All things are possible through you Lord.

I declare that I will not allow the mind of the flesh to rule but instead I will crucify my flesh so that God's mind will rule in the decisions I make and in every area of my life. My mind is renewed; I think higher thoughts those that are pure, good, lovely and honest. I am successful. In fact, success follows me. I am a leader and not a follower.

I am a chosen vessel of God, called, chosen, appointed and anointed to do His will. Nothing will stop me because I know who I am...I am a 5-fold officer, a prophetic prayer warrior, a marketplace leader, a global influencer and a game changer. I am destined to win. Prayer is the key to my destiny and success and I know without it I can do nothing.

Prayer

Lord make me sensitive to your voice at all times. Give me eyes so that I may see, ears so that I may hear and a heart to comprehend your will for my life. Obedience is key and like Hannah, let me pray without ceasing until I see your promises manifest in my life. Like Samuel, I desire to take my call to serve you seriously. Keep me mindful of your promises. Let me always be able to discern the correct times and seasons for my life. Thank you Lord for calling me into the kingdom for a such a time as this, Father release the angels that have been assigned to war on my behalf and those who have been assigned to bring increase, wealth, prosperity and good success into my life. In Jesus' name! Amen.

PROPHETIC WORDS

2014: THE YEAR OF COVENANT BLESSINGS

RECOMPENSE AND RECOVERY FOR THE RIGHTEOUS

This is the year of recompense and recovery for the righteous. The Lord is calling His people into the Ark of his Covenant, where he will pour out unprecedented favor and blessings to those who have honored their covenant with him. These blessings have been set aside for people who have been committed, dedicated, faithful, and relentless in their service for him. Our God is a covenant God who keeps his promises to his people and he will vindicate the righteous and punish the wicked. I heard the Lord say: *to my covenant people, I will give you understanding to know and believe my Word, memories to retain it and hearts to live it. Courage to profess it and the power to perform it, for my Word shall go out from among you and it shall not return void but, it shall accomplish that which it was sent to accomplish, thus saith the Lord.*

There will be a great outpouring of God's spirit over the earth making the ministration of the gospel so effectual that there, shall be a mighty increase in the spreading of the knowledge of Jesus Christ to many people. The Lord will use the liberal media and world news to create more controversial platforms of discussion to spread the gospel to a lost and dying people; causing his hand of grace to be extended to hearer's as he ushers in a harvest of souls. The presence of God shall visit his people like never before, filling every empty place with his glory. "But the time is coming when the earth shall be filled with the knowledge of the glory of The Lord as the waters cover the sea." (Habakkuk 2:14 Amp.)

INCREASE, INCREASE, INCREASE

Increase, increase, increase. I heard God say, *"I am bestowing double honor and double favor upon those who have stood in the face of their enemies, never wavering in their faith."* It will be like the story of Mordecai in (Esther 3:5-6 Amp.) "When Haman saw that Mordecai did not bow down or do him reverence he was very angry. But he scorned laying hands only on Mordecai, so since they had told him Mordecai's nationality, Haman sought to destroy all the Jews, the people of Mordecai, throughout the whole kingdom of Ahasuerus." Like Mordecai, there have been things that came against you because of your choice to stand with God but even as the story goes in Esther 6:1-9, it will be your story as well. The Lord said that *"the enemy that plotted to hang you shall be hung and the pit that was dug for you shall they fall in."* The Lord will promote and parade the righteous throughout the city and your family will rejoice knowing that their recompense has come.

DOUBLE SEVEN

$7+7 = 14$. Seven is the number of God that symbolizes world impact, sovereignty and absoluteness. It is the completion and fulfillment of cycles. It is the seven continents of the world being doubly infused with the supernatural power of God ruling from the heavens evading the earth. The sound over the earth has shifted blowing winds of acceleration with great manifestation positioning the church to take on its kingdom assignment to establish Joseph store houses. These kingdom governmental agencies (Joseph storehouses) will spring up in many cities to impact communities by meeting the needs of people according to a righteous and lawful kingdom code. The Lord will build and supply his resource centers with great substance to be distributed among those whom he is gathering into his ark of protection in these last days..

APOSTOLIC STRATEGY

The Lord is pouring out (downloading) Apostolic strategy on the leaders he is raising up in this hour to provide heavenly solutions to resolve every problem and circumstance. These Apostolic strategies will help them accomplish the work he has given them (with sweat less victory). I heard the Lord say that he shall redeem time on your behalf and things that were lost and even misplaced shall be recovered to you in double. The Lord will download heaven's intelligence to his leaders to work new technologies and extend greater resources to cause your work load to become lighter. These are the days of working smarter and not harder. The Spirit of God will cause "your few" to become mighty and "your little" to become much. He is raising up a Gideon's army in your camp to position your house for Apostolic rule in order to access the nations. We will experience a great leaping forth from the winds of acceleration forging us ahead.

Word of the Lord given by:
Prophet Cynthia Thompson
Jesus People Proclaim International Church
December 30, 2013

THE POWER OF A PROPHETIC MINDSET

The Prophetic Word Concerning Israel and the Things to Come June 18, 2014

The Lord spoke to me concerning war that is upon us and he said it is very important that we understand the times we are in and move swiftly to put things in place before 2016 for the outpouring that is coming beginning in the month of July. The four blood moons were a prophetic sign to the spiritual and natural Israel. We must put the blood over our lives dying to our selfish agendas and our self promoting ways. When the blood moons show up they prophetically declare to God's people that it is a time of crossing over and coming out of bondage and captivity however, with it comes persecution and death.

I didn't understand why he spoke to me 7/7/14 which is 7+7+7+7. This will be the beginning of everything; the four blood moons and the four 7's have all aligned. The four 7's are representative of the symbol Hitler wore on his arm. He killed and persecuted the Jews. The spirit of the anti-Christ and the "anti- God of Abraham, Isaac, Jacob" will make its move against both spiritual Israel and natural Israel. These spirits recognize the kingdom shift that has taken place and with this shift it brings in new economic rulers. The Lord showed me that Israel will respond to Iran and this will spark a war around the middle or end of 2015 (which has also been marked for the reappearing of the blood moons). I asked the Lord to explain and he said, he will cause them to advance and not back down from war; for the Lord shall be with His people and bring us into victory. Nation after nation will turn their backs and become angry against Israel-including America- which will be the last to leave Israel, but they will leave as well.

This will fulfill the prophecy that all nations shall come against Israel (Zechariah 12:3). It will also cause God's elite army to rise and take their new positions as the Lord drives out the old guards and sets the new guards in place to disburse a new allotment of resources that will be made available through end-time "Joseph Store Houses." God will use economic crisis and famine to cause brothers to find each other from distance lands. This is when we will see the Bride of Christ, made up of many nations, Jews and Gentiles, joining together for the two houses shall be made one and we will stand in unity to defeat the enemy.

The Lord said, "Focus on the building of the Glory Domes" which is his end-time Ark of safety and he will lead you to the Joseph's that will be storing up resources to replenish the land. The Lord will send us (righteous believers) double in this season to put in the Ark. Just as he told Noah to put the double or two of every kind in the Ark he built, so that there may be more than enough to take care of his people in this shift. The kingdom of darkness has focused on taking the gold, but I heard The Lord say, "for I shall give not only the gold in abundance to my people but those that wait upon me shall receive my Glory and the fire that comes with it, that they may be fully equipped to do my work in the earth." In these days ahead, what would have taken you years to accomplish, the Lord shall do it in one day, for these are the days of the supernatural outpouring and my people will move in supernatural power just like my son Jesus did and they will fulfill the Word spoken of the greater works that will follow those who believe.

Works Cited

[1] "conscious." Merriam-Webster.com. 2011. http://www.merriam-webster.com

[2] "unconscious." Merriam-Webster.com. 2011. http://www.merriam-webster.com

[3] "subconscious." Merriam-Webster.com. 2011. http://www.merriam-webster.com

[4] "The Human Mind – How Does It All Work?" Mindset Habits. 20 May 2010. Web.

[5] "metamorphosis." Merriam-Webster.com. 2011. http://www.merriam-webster.com

[6] "wrestling." Merriam-Webster.com. 2011. http://www.merriam-webster.com

[7] Price, Paula A. The Prophet's Dictionary: The Ultimate Guide to Supernatural Wisdom. 2006., pg. 463 entry 1238: realm

[8] "power." Blue Letter Bible. Web. 13 Aug. 2013

[9] Sparks, T. A. "What Prophetic Ministry Is." Prophetic Ministry: A Classic Study of the Nature of a Prophet. 2. Print

[10] "cultivation." Merriam-Webster.com. 2011. http://www.merriam-webster.com

[11] "mindset." Merriam-Webster.com. 2011. http://www.merriam-webster.com

WORDS CITED

12 "perspective." Merriam-Webster.com. 2011. http://www.merriam-webster.com

13 "dispensation." Merriam-Webster.com. 2011. http://www.merriam-webster.com

14 Price, Paula A. The Prophet's Dictionary: The Ultimate Guide to Supernatural Wisdom. 2006., pg. 212 entry 502: familiar spirit

15 Price, Paula A. The Prophet's Dictionary: The Ultimate Guide to Supernatural Wisdom. 2006., pg. 386 entry 1033: portal

16 Price, Paula A. The Prophet's Dictionary: The Ultimate Guide to Supernatural Wisdom. 2006., pg. 546 entry 1474: supernatural

17 Price, Paula A. The Prophet's Dictionary: The Ultimate Guide to Supernatural Wisdom. 2006., pg. 467 entry 1247: revelatory

18 Price, Paula A. The Prophet's Dictionary: The Ultimate Guide to Supernatural Wisdom. 2006., pg. 467 entry 1246: revelation

19 Price, Paula A. The Prophet's Dictionary: The Ultimate Guide to Supernatural Wisdom. 2006., pg. 404 entry 1084: prophetic accuracy

20 "authority ." Merriam-Webster.com. 2011. http://www.merriam-webster.com

21 Price, Paula A. The Prophet's Dictionary: The Ultimate Guide to Supernatural Wisdom. 2006., pg. 526 entry 1412 sphere

22 Price, Paula A. The Prophet's Dictionary: The Ultimate Guide to Supernatural Wisdom. 2006., pg. 433 entry 1157: prophetic prayer